Searching for My Mountain

SEARCHING FOR MY MOUNTAIN

ISBN **978-1-935786-86-3**

Printed in the United States of America by
St. Clair Publications
P. O. Box 726
Mc Minnville, TN 37111-0726

Cover Design by Eric St. Clair; Front Cover Photo by Terri Davis

Searching for My Mountain

Terri Thomas St. Clair

Edited by Stan St. Clair

SEARCHING FOR MY MOUNTAIN

Contents

SEARCHING FOR MY MOUNTAIN

Searching for my Mountain

The Mountains Trilogy

Book Two

Chapter One

It had been a month since Daniel and I were married. The time had passed by so swiftly. We had taken a week and a half honeymoon in Hawaii and our time together had been marvelous. I had totally recovered from all my health problems stemming from the blood clot. I had never felt stronger. I could have stayed here in my new house and been just as happy as I was in Hawaii. Not that Hawaii wasn't wonderful, but anywhere with Daniel would have been perfect to me. Mandy is like a kid in a candy shop with the new house. She spoils Daniel and me so much. She lets me do all the cooking I want to, and tries very hard to let me have the run of the house. She's always asking me how I want things done.

When we got back I found a realtor and put my house on the market. It wasn't doing me any good sitting there empty. I was back to the mountains for good. Chris decided to go ahead and sell his home, so both of us were using the same agent. He had fallen in love with the mountains and the people he had begun to call his patients. I was surprised that my home had sold so quickly.

Two of the doctors that helped Daniel when I was sick were also coming on board, as expected. Daniel had been so busy since coming back. He tried his best to be home early but sometimes it was just impossible. We had begun our marriage in the little white chapel, and we became members right after we returned from our honeymoon. We had grown up going to church there. Who would have thought we would be coming back as husband and wife. Daniel took time every morning to have devotions with me. Our prayer time was so precious.

I hadn't gone to my mother's house since she died. I knew I had to, but for some reason I hadn't been able to. I wanted to wait until Daniel could go with me. Anna Belle had gone over and cleaned out the refrigerator, and had thrown out all the perishable food. So now the hard part was up to me. I must go through her personal things and decide what to do with them. I guess I just wasn't strong enough physically or emotionally until now.

We tried to make time on Sunday afternoon to visit with Daniel's family. Mom Scott always had a big dinner after church and we were always invited to come by. Chris would join us sometimes. We became his extended family. The Scotts adopted him along with me.

Grandmother Scott gave us a running assessment of how the population viewed the new health care for the community. There were mixed reviews, of course. Some were more easily convinced than others. Grandmother Scott remained in excellent health. She was faithful in her checkups with Daniel.

I had a surprise in store for Daniel when he came in from work that day. I was going to offer him the profit from the sale of my house to further the health care here.

I thought a long time about converting a recreational vehicle into a mobile medical clinic. It didn't seem like a farfetched idea. I'm sure with all the input from Chris we could make a real impact. With all the hidden hollows in the mountains there where so many not willing or able to come to the clinic to get needed help.

They continued on with the roots and herbs passed from generation to generation. Some worked well, but some not only couldn't cure, but could kill. With the clinic well staffed now, I thought we could travel together, doctor and nurse, to those isolated places and take the care to them. I hadn't mentioned this to anyone except the Lord.

Daniel had a gazebo built behind our house with a swing inside. There was a path winding down the hill to it. We would sit there sometimes in the evening and listen to the birds sing in the trees around us. It had a beautiful view of the valley below us. We could see wisps of smoke curl up from the chimneys. I would sit sometimes and try to imagine the wood cook stove preparing the evening meal or perhaps a wood stove warming the home itself.

I would let my mind would wander back to the times I had sat by the fire while Mama cooked supper. The wonderful dinners she would prepare brought pleasant memories. She could make a perfect cake in that old wood stove.

I was waiting for Daniel in the gazebo. I told Mandy to send him down as soon as he came in. I had set there and rehearsed what I was going to say. I went over and over it in my mind. I had the envelope in my hand with the check in it from where I sold the house. I was so excited I could hardly wait. I closed my eyes and willed myself to calm down. I heard the birds sing and the rustle of the wind through the woods, but it still didn't calm my anxiousness.

I felt two hands come over my eyes and I knew it was Daniel.

"Guess who?" he asked.

"I hope it's my husband," I returned.

He came around and set down beside me. He leaned over and gave me a sweet kiss. I looked forward to this time of day when I would feel his lips on mine again. I still couldn't get enough of him. What sweet times we had together.

"What's wrong?" he asked, taking a seat beside me.

"Why?"

"Well you don't usually ask me to meet you in the swing. Do we have a problem?"

"I hope you don't think of it as a problem," I said, smiling at him.

"Let's see, are we pregnant yet?" he said, looking at me expectantly.

"I don't think so," I said. It's something just as special, I think."

"Okay, I'm through guessing."

I handed him the envelope. He took it and held it for a moment before he opened it up. He took the check out and held it in his hand.

"This is from where you sold your home. I knew it was due to come."

"I want to give it to you," I said.

"Elizabeth, it's sweet of you to offer me money, but I have enough for the both of us to live on, and more."

"Well, it's not exactly for us to live on, but it's far more special. Let me tell you what I've been thinking about."

"Oh no, you've been thinking! That could be dangerous," he said, teasing me.

"As I was saying, I was thinking maybe we could get a recreational vehicle and equip it as a mobile clinic. We could travel into the remote places of Virginia and West Virginia to care for those people that wouldn't come to us. What do you think?" I asked excitedly.

He put his arm around me and pulled me close to him and kissed me.

"This is all kind of sudden, but I think it is a great idea. I've thought about the same thing from time to time, but I wasn't sure how we could do it. With this we could do a great deal. I've been so busy trying to get the clinic established I haven't been able to give it my attention. Who would run this mobile hospital?" he said, turning to look at me.

"Well, that's my next idea. I thought the two of us could. I could be your nurse. You've told me often enough that you would be the doctor and I would be the nurse."

"You? This is a surprise. I kind of thought you might start back, but I didn't want to rush you. You know you don't need to work."

"But I want to. I have all this training and people need me."

"I think we could pull this off. Let me sleep on it, and tomorrow I'll run it by Chris. Come here and give me a kiss."

We sat for a long time swinging and kissing. I could never get tired of his love. I remembered the key that Mama had given me and decided to bring it up him.

"Daniel, do you remember the key Mama gave to me the night she died?"

"Yes, I was waiting for you to bring it up. I figured when you were ready we could go over to her house and see if we could find something this key will fit."

"I've been thinking about it, and I think I'm ready to see whatever it is. Maybe we could go tonight. We haven't turned off the electricity yet. Would you like that?"

"Yeah, I think I would. Let's go eat supper then we can go over."

He got to his feet and pulled me to mine. He drew me close to him and kissed me long and tenderly.

"I look forward to you all day. I can't wait to get home to you and this," he said, kissing me again.

"I hope this honeymoon stage never ends," he said, smiling at me.

"We better go, dinner will be cold."

We made our way up the hill to the house. Mandy had dinner ready and waiting.

"I'll be right there," he said, heading for the stairs. "I want to go change right quick."

As soon as we had finished dinner we headed to my mom's house. I really dreaded this trip and had put it off as long as possible. It would be the first time I had been back since my Thanksgiving trip. That seemed a lifetime ago.

"I really dread this. You remember me telling you about the feeling I've had about this place?"

"Are you talking about the unknown fear?"

"Yeah, it's something I've felt here for as long as I can remember. I think that's why I wanted to get away. This is it Daniel," I said, holding up the little brass key.

"I'm holding my fear in my hand. It's like holding a hot coal. I would like to throw it away but I know I have to face whatever it is that this key fits."

"We'll do this together. If you want me to, I'll look first and tell you what I find."

"No, we'll look together," I said with a weak smile.

SEARCHING FOR MY MOUNTAIN

We got out of the car and walked hand in hand to the front porch.

The last time Daniel walked me to this door we weren't even engaged, I thought. He put the key in the door and it opened easily.

"Here we go," he said, going in before me.

He fumbled inside the door for the light switch. I slipped under his arm and easily found it. I had used it a million times. The overhead light came on and illumined the room. The big clock no longer ticked. It was eerily quite. I don't know why, but I felt that had to wind the clock. I had never heard it be silent. It's as if it had died along with its inhabitants. There was no one else to stand sentry over. I had the door opened to wind it, but decided to let "him" remain mute.

I wandered into the kitchen. The room that once seemed so bright and cheery now seemed to be cold and uninviting. The refrigerator door was left open so it wouldn't mildew. How precious Anna Belle had been to have taken over the things that I should have done.

I walked over to Mom's chair by the window and sat down. I reached over and turned on the table lamp. Its light seemed to soften the harshness of the overhead ceiling light. Tears escaped my eyes and ran down my cheeks.

"She loved this chair," I said, wiping my eyes.

"Sweetheart, do you want me to go into her room and look for something this key will fit?" he said tenderly to me.

I shook my head and extended my hand toward him. He reached out and pulled me to my feet and into his arms. He held me close.

"There's nothing here that can hurt you."

He took my hand and led me down the hall to the bedroom. I noticed Anna had made Mama's bed and everything was neat and in its place.

I opened her closet and saw all her clothing hanging just as she left it. Waiting for her to come and wear them. I pulled one of her sweaters to my face catching a faint sent of her lavender sachet. I held it to me just as I had David's clothing, hoping to feel her closeness once again. But in both cases, it was merely a garment, their lives were gone. My mind went back to the day I saw her in heaven. How happy she was there. I must make myself remember that day and not the emptiness of this house.

"I think I need to get a light and a stepstool so I can check back in the corner of the closet."

I walked about the room while he went in search of a stool. Her Bible lay on the simple table beside her bed. The cover was worn from countless hours of holding it and reading it. How often she must have held it as she prayed for my healing from all the grief I was suffering. She needed me and I wouldn't come to her. How selfish of me, I thought. I picked it up and pressed it to my chest as if to somehow feel the prayers she had prayed.

"Honey, I finally found a flashlight that worked. I couldn't find a stool, so I brought the next best thing, a chair," he said, pulling it up to the closet.

16

"Do you need me to hold the light?" I asked.

"That would help."

I stood on my tiptoes and shined the light in the direction he was looking.

"It would help if I knew what I was looking for," he said, stretching on his toes and reaching toward the far corners of the closet.

"Did she say closet?" he asked.

"I can't remember." I replied.

"It's not on the top shelf." he said, removing the chair.

I got down on my hands and knees to look in the back. I removed shoes and various other items on the floor, but there was nothing with a key hole.

"Maybe it's under the bed," Daniel said, getting on his hands and knees to look.

"I don't see anything that a key would fit in," he said, sitting on the floor beside me.

"The clock uses a key, but it has its own," he muttered to himself.

"Maybe it would be in one of her drawers. She could have hidden it under her clothing," I said, getting to my feet.

I started checking in her chest of drawers, slowly and meticulously moving things. I didn't have time to mourn as I handled her things. We searched all the drawers to no avail. Daniel had gone through one of her other dressers while I was going though another.

"How big do you think this thing is?" Daniel asked me.

"Your guess is as good as mine," I returned.

"Where do we look now? Unless she has it in a secret chamber, it isn't in this room," Daniel said.

"Oh Daniel, I don't have a clue," I said, exasperated. "I don't think she would have put it in my room, but where would she have put it?"

"Maybe it could be in the guest room, let's start looking there," I said, heading down the hall.

The room was neat as a pin. It was a beautiful little room. Mama always called it 'Jonny's room. I assumed it was his nursery during his brief life here.

The furniture in the room was sparse but pretty. There was a large closet in the room with clothing still hanging there. She would transfer seasonal clothing from one to the other for the convenience of it.

"Well, I guess I need to get the chair and flashlight from the other room," he said, heading out of the room.

There was a small chest of drawers in the corner. I would go through it if he couldn't find what we were looking for in the closet.

Once again, Daniel climbed on the chair to investigate the contents of the closet.

"Libby, I'll be darned if I see anything that looks like it has a lock. Think like your mom, and see what pops up."

"That's a hard one," I said, smiling at him.

"Okay, Lord, you know what this thing is, so impress on my mind where to look," I prayed out loud.

"I think he is the only one that knows right now. Maybe he will send it floating through the air and right into our hands."

"Daniel, be serious!"

"I am," he said with a chuckle.

"You'll be surprised if God sends me an answer."

"Actually, I wouldn't be. I've seen him do some mighty miraculous things, like bring you to me."

"Yeah, that was a miracle, wasn't it?" I replied.

"I'm going to go out and check the shelves on the porch. Sit in your mom's chair and see if she sends you a message," he said.

I sat there with my eyes closed, trying to imagine where in the world she could have put this locked item. I suddenly felt lips on mine, jarring me to the present.

"Boo!" Daniel said, laughing and startling me.

19

"I was trying to think. Don't do that!" I said, irritated with him.

"I'm sorry; I didn't mean to scare you. I just couldn't help it. Well, I guess I did mean to, didn't I. Let me make up for it," he said, kissing me tenderly."

"I'll forgive you this time. I gather you didn't find anything with a keyhole in it."

"Nope, I came up empty. She sure knew how to keep a secret. I guess she wouldn't put it somewhere you would accidentally stumble onto it," he said, thinking out loud.

"What about the attic where she kept the Christmas decorations? Maybe it could be there," Daniel said.

"Let's go look," I said, getting up.

"But how will we know when we find it?" Daniel asked, pulling down the steps to the attic.

"The key will fit," I said, laughing at him.

"Don't be a smarty pants," he replied.

There was one light swinging down at the end of a long electrical cord. Daddy had it put in so he could see where to work up there.

There was stuff spread everywhere. Where would we start looking? I wondered.

"Daniel, look, over there in the corner! It's a trunk," I said, climbing over Christmas decorations to get to it.

SEARCHING FOR MY MOUNTAIN

It was an old humpback trunk, with tin arched over the top. There was a design in it made by a tin punch. Leather bands were stretched over the top, holding it in place. The locking system was rusted and I couldn't budge it.

"Let me see if I can pry it open," he said, working on it with his bare hands.

"I think I'm going to need something that can give me leverage. Look around and see if you see anything I could use," he said, still trying to get it to loosen.

I found an old screwdriver that had been discarded many years ago.

"Here, maybe this will work," I said, handing it to him.

He took the old rusty implement and began to push it in the lock. It slipped and went into his knuckle.

"Ouch!" he said, slinging his hand in the air. "That hurt."

"Hold still and let me see," I said, taking his hand in mine. "That's what you get for scaring me awhile ago."

"What, sticking a rusty screwdriver in my finger? That doesn't seem like an even trade to me."

"When did you have your last tetanus shot, Dr. Scott? You just might have to have one."

"Don't go getting medical on me, Nurse Scott," he said, holding his right hand in his left.

"Let me see," I said, taking his hand in mine. "Look, it's just a scratch, a Band-Aid and a kiss will make it all better. I promise. See, it's barely bleeding."

"Kiss it now," he said, holding it to my lips.

"No! It has blood on it. I'll kiss it when the Band-Aid's on."

"Good friend you are," he said with mock pain.

"Does it hurt as bad now?"

"No, not now," he said, taking inventory of his wound."

"Then can you try again?"

"Woman, don't you have any mercy?"

"I love you sweetheart," I said, giving him a little kiss on the cheek.

"I want you to kiss my finger," he said, teasing me. "I'm not going to work again until you do it."

"Give it here." I said in exasperation.

I kissed his finger above the wound that was now turning purple. Is that close enough?"

"Yeah, that'll do," he said, smiling at me.

He proceeded to pry the lock a little more gingerly this time. It finally gave way through the rust that had gathered over the years.

"No one has been in here for ages," Daniel said, opening the lid.

Inside was a menagerie of things. I gently picked up the articles one by one to look at them. On top, in tissue paper, was the suit that Daddy had worn at my wedding. It was the first and only time I saw him in a suit. I knew he wasn't buried in it, but I never had asked her what she did with it.

"Look, Daniel, this is the suit Daddy wore for mine and David's wedding." Mama had packed it away with such care. I laid it aside and proceeded to look further for the mysterious item which the little gold key would fit.

"Look, Daniel, I found a box in the bottom of the trunk," I said excitedly.

"Does it have a key hole?" he inquired.

"No, it's tied with a ribbon."

"Then I know that's not what we're looking for," he said.

"I know, but it may hold treasure," I said, picking it up.

I gently pulled the bow and released the ribbon from the box. Inside was a long gown and a tiny bonnet. I held up the garment that, on closer inspection, looked like it was hand-stitched. The once white linen now was spotted yellow.

I held it close to me and remembered the little boy I saw in heaven. Now I could put a face to my little brother.

His birth certificate was neatly laid in bottom of the box. There was a little spray of brown hair tied with a ribbon, and taped to it.

"These were Jonathan's things," I said. "I'm surprised she left them in this old trunk."

"Maybe they were too painful to look at," Daniel replied.

"I wonder if Daddy went to his christening. He hated the church at the time Jonathan was a baby," I said quizzically.

"Maybe he did. He seemed to love him a lot, from what your mom said."

"Daniel, can we move this trunk to our house? I would like to refinish it someday."

"Sure, but does it have to be tonight?"

"No, you don't have to tonight, but sometime soon."

"Well, we need to keep searching for the elusive thing with a small key hole."

We continued to search the attic, but to no avail. We went back down the steps to hear knocking at the kitchen door.

"I wonder who that could be," I said, going to answer it.

Anna Belle was standing there, looking in the window pane of the door. I opened it and invited her in.

"I saw some lights on up here and wanted to make sure there weren't no haints in here," she said, looking at me wide-eyed.

"Do you mean to tell me you would actually come up here to find out? I think I would have just stayed at my house and wondered," I said with a chuckle.

"I ain't never been afraid to go see what things are, thata way you don't have to be afeared of what ya don't know."

"I think that makes sense," I said, still a little perplexed.

"I'm glad it was only you, 'Lis'beth," she said.

"Me too!" Daniel injected.

"I'm glad to see yer doin' better from you sickness and all. You and Doctor Daniel sure looked purty at yer weddin'. Yer mama would'a been so proud."

"We're going through some of Mama's things. We just came down from the attic. Actually, we're looking for something this key fits."

Her eyes widened. "She showed me that key one day. She said, 'One day 'Lis'beth is gonna want to know things I cain't tell her now, and this here key will unlock the box.'"

"So it's a box?" I asked excitedly.

25

"Yeah, I've knowed about it, but I ain't never seed it," she said, scratching her head.

"Do you know where she kept it?" Daniel inquired.

"This ole' brain just cain't call up things like it used too."

"Think, Anna Belle, think!" I interjected.

"Well, a long time ago she showed me a place in one of her drawers she kept 'portant stuff in."

"Could you show us?"

"I don't know if I can, but I'll try."

We all traipsed single file down the narrow hall, Daniel leading the way, stopping in Mama's room.

"Let me think. Wher' was that thing?" she murmured to herself. "I think it was in that chester drawer right there," she said, pointing.

I felt downcast. "Anna, we've already looked through there. Are you sure though? "

"I think I am. I'm almost positive it's the one. She brung me back one day and showed me. She took a little key on a ribbon and opened it."

"What did the box look like?" Daniel and I asked in unison.

"It was a wooden box, much like one of them jewe'ry boxes."

"Was it tall or flat?" Daniel inquired.

"I think it was long and flat, so's it would fit the drawer good."

"Is that all you can remember?" I asked her, trying to will her to recall.

"Maybe if'n I go look, maybe it would jar this ole noggin," she said with a chuckle. "If ya don't min', that is."

"No, please, go look all you want," I said, encouraging her to go ahead.

"Ya got to remember, "Lisbeth, it's been nigh on twenty year since I seed it. She kept tellin' me it was to be a deep secert where she put it. She said you musn't find it till she was…"

"I know, passed. Keep thinking, Anna this is so important," I said, encouraging her further.

"I'm tryin', I'm tryin'." She said with a perplexed look crossing her brow. I jest cain't 'member what it was she did."

She went through all the drawers one by one.

"I guess she done put it som'ers else. I'm sorry I couldn't he'p more. I sure wanted too."

"It's okay," I said, hugging her. "I'm sure Daniel and I will find it. At least we know it's a flat box," I said with at sigh.

"Well, I guess I'll head on down the holler since I know there ain't no haints up hyer."

Her snaggled teeth were prominent as she threw her head back to laugh.

"No haints, just saints," Daniel added with a hearty laugh.

"I know what ya mean, Doctor Daniel, I know what ya mean," she said, still chuckling to herself.

"Bye," I said as she headed out the door.

"Be careful and don't fall," Daniel called after her.

"I got my flashlight, I'll be okay. I walked these hollers fer years. Bye now."

"I'm sorry, honey; I knew you had your hopes up high. But you know God will show us where it is," he said, comforting me.

"Why don't we go home and get some rest. We can come back over here tomorrow and look some more," he said hugging me. "We'll get the trunk then, too."

I went into the bedroom to turn off the light. It hadn't been long ago since I lay in bed with her and shared with her about mine and Daniel's first intimate moments.

We had everything turned off and ready to leave when we heard a knock on the door again.

"It's sure busy here tonight," Daniel said, going to see who was there.

"Its jus' me again," Anna said. "I was a goin' down the holler and I kinda remembered sumpthin' about the bottom movin'. I don't know if it will he'p any, but I thought I better come tell ya."

"The bottom of the box moved?" I implored.

"No, not the box, the drawer," she replied.

"Oh, my God!" Daniel said, running down the hall. "It has to be a false bottom."

I ran after Daniel, with Anna close on my heels.

"Anna, which drawer was it?" Daniel said hurriedly.

"I'm sorry, I don't 'member. Ya got to 'member how long ago it was," she said, scratching her head and looking puzzled again.

"Just dump the things on to the bed," I said to Daniel.

We started with the top one. Having dumped it, he pecked all around to see if it sounded hollow.

"It's not this one," he said, proceeding to check the others.

"Say a little prayer, sweetie this is the last one," he said, dumping its contents onto the bed.

He began his pecking process, being careful of his bruised knuckle.

He looked at me with a wide grin. "This is it. We've found the treasure!"

"How do you get it open?" I asked.

"I was just getting ready to ask you the same question," he returned.

"Don't go lookin' at me. I's sure don't know nothin' 'bout it," Anna chirped.

Daniel worked and worked to no avail. Sweat was pouring down his brow.

"I've never seen one of these before," he said, exasperated. "One would think it would be much simpler."

"Maybe that's why they call it a secret drawer," I said, smiling at him childishly.

"Are you being a smarty pants again, Mrs. Scott?" he asked.

"I'm just kidding."

"Who would know how one of these things works?" he murmured as he worked.

"Maybe someone that grew up in the era that Mama did."

I saw a little light go off in his head. His eyes brightened. "My dad or mom might know."

He went into the living room to call his dad.

"No phone hookup," he said dejectedly.

"I guess we could take the drawer by their house," I said.

"It's getting late. Maybe we could take the drawer to our house and call him in the morning," he replied.

"That's a good idea. I'm getting tired and I'm sure you are. Plus we have to fix your war wound," I said, smiling at him.

"Anna, thanks a million. We couldn't have done it without you."

"I jus' wish I coulda knowed how that thing worked."

"Do you want us to drop you off by your house?" Daniel asked.

"No sir, I jus' walk. Thanks anyway. I be prayin' ya get that thing fixed," she said as she went out the door.

Chapter Two

It was well after midnight when we returned home. Daniel took the drawer and put it in the garage.

"We'll get it open tomorrow even if we have to cut the thing in two," he said reassuringly.

I went into the bedroom and changed into my night clothes.

"Honey, I'm going to take a quick shower. I feel grimy after the venture into the attic. I need to wash my cut out, too," he said, examining it again.

"I'll kiss it after you get the Band-Aid on it."

"I won't be long. Don't go to sleep before I get there," he said, kissing me on the tip of my nose.

"I have to clean my face and brush the dust out of my hair. I'm sure I'll still be awake by the time you're through."

I had just slipped into my side of the bed when Daniel finished. He held his newly bandaged finger up for me to kiss. I took his hand gently in mine and kissed his finger.

"Is that better, sweetheart?" I said, looking into his eyes.

"I think I need a few more kisses."

He reached over and turned off the lamp by his bed.

"Come here, sweetie, let me hold you a little. Have I told you today how much I love you?"

"Umm I think you might have, but tell me again. I love to hear it."

"I love you more than the stars in the sky and the sand on the seashore."

"I love you that much and more."

"You can't love me more than I love you. I have to think up something else."

"We love each other the same," I said, kissing his neck.

"Oh, Mrs. Scott, show me how much you love me," he said, pulling me close to him.

"I think I showed you once before, that should be enough," I said, teasing him.

"I have short term memory loss. I need to be shown often. In a lifetime I couldn't get tired of this."

"A lifetime is a long time."

"I know, isn't that great?"

"Yeah."

"Daniel?"

"Shhh, no more talking, just love me," he said, claiming his love from me once again.

I felt Daniel gently shaking me, and calling my name.

"Daniel... what do you want?" I said, rubbing the sleep from my eyes.

"Look...! Set up and look at what I have."

"I know what you have, now let me sleep."

"Silly girl, wake up, I've got something to show you."

I roused on one elbow, shielding my eyes from the light he had turned on.

"What time is it?" I said, straining to see the clock.

"It's five o'clock."

"What are you doing? It's Saturday, you don't work."

He held his hands out in front of me. Lying in them was a long brown box.

"Is this 'the box'?" I asked.

"Yes, my darling, it is 'the box'," he said. "I couldn't sleep thinking about that false bottom. So I got out of bed and I've been working on it ever since. Finally, I worked it out, and here it is."

"You couldn't stand it, could you? You were always like that, you know. You couldn't stand to be defeated, and I'm so glad you couldn't. Come here and let me thank you."

I kissed him as he handed me the box. My fingers traced the chiseled carving on the top. Here it was: my past, present and future, closed up in this wooden box, no longer than twelve or thirteen inches long and maybe two inches deep. Perhaps it held the secrets of my life, possibly the name of my grandmother whom I needed to find. I held it on my lap, wanting to, but yet afraid to use the key.

"What are you thinking?" Daniel asked, as he crawled back into bed beside me.

"I have a myriad of thoughts. Once I open this box there is no turning back, and there will no more Elizabeth Ann Edwards. I'll know the truth, and the truth shall set me free. Then again, maybe there isn't anything in there that will help me find the grandmother that gave me away.

"Do you really want to find this grandmother? After all, she sent you away," Daniel said tenderly.

"Daniel, I've got to tell you a story," I said, still caressing the wooden box with my fingertips.

"Okay, but do you have to tell me before you open the box?"

"Yeah, it has to do with opening this," I said, looking at the box. "I've wanted to share this with you for a long time, but the right moment hadn't come."

"It's five in the morning, are you sure this is the time?" he questioned.

"I've been working all night to find this, and you're not going to open it?" he said disappointedly.

"First, I've got to tell this to you. Remember the time when I was in a coma, and I told you I had been with David?"

"Yeah, but what does this have to do with the box," he said quietly.

"It has everything to do with this box."

"Your dreams have something to do with what is in here?" he inquired.

"Oh, but Daniel, it wasn't a dream! That's why I need to tell you what happened before I open this box. It will be a validation to where I was when I was in my coma. If what I *think* is there, really is, I'll know for sure where I was."

"You're confusing me. All I remember you saying was that you were with David, so silly me, I thought you must have been dreaming, after all you just said you were with a dead man."

"There was so much more that happened while I was there. I saw David, yes, but I also saw…" I was almost

36

afraid to go on. "Promise me you won't think I'm stupid or crazy," I interjected.

He turned my face, so I was looking directly into his eyes.

"I would never, ever think that. I'm ready to hear whatever it is you feel you need to tell me at...what time is it now..." he squinted to see the clock by my bedside, 5:30 it is now. Even though I've worked all night to get that puzzle drawer open, I'm ready."

"Before I open this, I feel I know some of the things I will find.

"When I was in my coma, it seemed as if I just woke from sleeping and was in a bright, beautiful place. I was in this field of flowers, and I turned and saw my mom and dad walking toward me. They had a little boy with them and they introduced me to him as my baby brother.

"They were so glad to see me. They held me in their arms, and kissed my face. I felt their touch. I could physically feel their arms around me. They were so young looking and healthy.

"I walked in the meadow, I swam in the River of Life, I met my brother, Jonathan, and my mother and twin sister."

I stole a look at his face as he understood what I had just told him. He just looked tenderly at me.

"I'm telling the truth, Daniel. It was as real as lying here beside you in bed. The reason I didn't stay with them is the silver cord never broke."

"A silver cord," he repeated. "Everything is still just a little bit fuzzy, but I'm listening."

"It seems that we are all tethered to this earthly body we live in by a silver cord. When the cord breaks, that's when we can't come back to earth. My cord never broke. I kept checking to make sure, but I couldn't see it. Only those that had crossed over could see it."

"I'm glad neither one of us can see it," he said, smiling at me.

"How come I feel like you're not taking me seriously?" I asked.

"Come here, sweetie," he said, pulling me closer to him. I do, or am *trying* to understand, if I sound like I'm not, forgive me," he requested.

"All right," I responded.

"Okay, let's take this one person at a time. You saw your brother? The one we saw the clothes for in the trunk? Is that right?"

"Right," I replied.

"See, I was listening."

"He was with my mother, and daddy. He was so cute, and seemed to be about eight years old. I can't remember him saying anything to me though, he just smiled at me. There was another woman with my mother, and she had a little girl with her. She seemed to be about the age of Jonathan. My mother told me she wanted me to meet my mother, my real mother," I said, hurriedly trying to get it all out.

"Slow down just a bit and sort the mother thing out for me."

"My mother that raised me, Mary Margaret, introduced me to my birth mother and my twin sister, Abby."

"Go on I'm following you," he said taking my hand in his.

"Okay, my mother's name is Rose and the little girl she had with her was Abby, my twin sister."

"Your mother mentioned that right before she died?"

"My mother, the real one, said she loved me very much and prayed for me the whole time she carried me in her womb. When she was in childbirth, things went badly and she and Abby died, and I lived. Why Daniel? Why was I chosen to live and Abby die? Why did God let me live and take their lives?"

"If I had that answer I wouldn't be on earth. I'm so glad he left you for me," he said gently.

"It seemed each one of them had their special time with me. When it was time for another to come, the one that was there disappeared somewhere. I wasn't with anyone of them very long except for..."

"Let me guess... could it have been David?" he said, shifting away from me.

39

"Yeah, it... I was so happy to see him. This is so difficult for me to tell you because I don't want to hurt your feelings."

"I'm the one that has you in the flesh, and I'm the one in bed with you right now, and I'm the one who made love to you a few hours ago. Look, I don't feel threatened by David. If I react sometimes, it's just because I know he shared with you the one thing I wish you had only shared with me, and if feel a little jealous. Then I remind myself that we will always share the same heart. Tell me whatever you need to, okay? I'm here for you.

"I told you before we married that anything you needed to say about David I was okay with. He was an integral part of your life. You loved him, and now you love me. I'm still adjusting, but I'm okay with it."

"He told me when he died in the emergency room, he was aware I was with him, and he saw me right before he...before he died." Unbidden tears slipped down my cheeks remembering the horrific scene.

Daniel drew me near to him and held me a little closer.

"It's okay, sweetie, you don't have to finish."

"But I do. He said he felt no pain; he wanted me to know that. He was there with me the night I dreamed he asked me to release him. Daniel, he was there just like I told you it happened in my dream!"

"I don't doubt that, because it was then that you felt free to be mine."

40

"My mother was so precious. She was beautiful. Her hair fell in cascades down around her shoulders. It was brunette, just like mine. She told me she loved me," I said, letting my tears flow freely. "She loved me, Daniel, my mother loved me."

"She would have to of loved you, that's why you're so sweet. Her loved rubbed off on you," he said, smiling at me.

"There was something so sad that she said to me. She told me my grandmother wasn't saved and I had to go find her. She said her mother's life was filled with abuse and bitterness. She, her mother, Ruth, never knew what happiness was; as a result she was a very bitter and angry woman."

"So the grandmother has a name?" Daniel inquired.

"She told me that right before she left me. David came up and whisked me away before I found out. He said I would have time with her later, but that was the last time I saw her until the bridge."

"What happened at the bridge?"

"I first need to tell you what happened at the water."

"Under the bridge?" he inquired.

"No, not the water under the bridge; the water in the meadow."

41

"So we're not at the bridge anymore, we're in the meadow?"

"Right, are you with me now?" I asked.

"I'm right with you. Go ahead," he returned.

"There was a river there in the meadow called the 'River of Life'. We sat beside the crystal water for a while with our feet dangling in. Then David suggested we go into the water, which we did. When we got out where it was getting really deep, I was afraid to go under. So he told me to try it, that in heaven we didn't have to breathe under water. I followed his lead and went under, and found that I felt very comfortable not breathing. Daniel, it was so wonderful. The temperature was perfect. We floated around in the water for a while then when we got out, we were perfectly dry."

"It sounds like it was something to behold. Then, what happened after you got out of the river?"

"He said he wanted to walk with me. We left the meadow and wandered through a forest. There was a path that ambled through it. Light filtered down through the limbs of the foliage and made beautiful patterns on the forest floor. The path we followed through the forest came out into a clearing and that was when I saw the bridge. It was white marble and arched over a body of water."

"Did you see your mother again, your birth mother, that is?" he asked.

"She stood on the other side of the bridge with my family and little sister, Abby. They were all waving and smiling at me.

"He said, 'it's time now for you to choose what you're going to do.' I said, 'you mean I can come with you?' And he answered, 'yes,' that it was my decision to make. I threw my arms around him and said of course I would go with him, because I loved him so much." I looked at Daniel and he had a pained expression on his face.

"You chose David?" he asked, with a hurt sound in his voice. "You chose not to come back to me?"

"Well, at first I did. You have to remember how much I loved him."

"Evidently you wanted him more than me=," he interjected.

"Who am I with, Daniel?" I said, becoming a bit irritated with him.

"Me, but you wanted to stay with him. Didn't you?"

"Let me finish the story. As I was starting across the bridge, my mother called out to me, 'Lis'beth, don't forget your grandmother.' Then I thought, if I don't go, who will? I knew if I crossed to the other side of the bridge, my cord would be broken. And then I heard you calling my name. You commanded me to look at you. So I turned and looked into your beautiful blue eyes. You told me not to look back, but to come to you. You said, 'don't take your eyes off mine, Libby,' and I didn't. When I ran into your arms you held me very tight to you. I did look back, but only once, and they all had gone. It was right after that, that the horrible pain rushed back into my body.

I woke up to you calling my name. I came back to you, Daniel, I could have stayed, but I came back to you."

Daniel had his fingers pressed to his eyes holding back the tears that were forming.

"I begged God for you, Elizabeth. Every day, I was in that chapel, asking God to give you back to me. It's funny that wherever you were, I was transported there to bring you back, and never knew. When you opened your eyes, I couldn't believe it for a moment. I thought I was dreaming."

"Neither of us was dreaming. I was transported to heaven for a time. I don't even know how long I was there, but I know I was there, and when I open this box I will find something there that will tell me all of this was not a dream."

"Are we ready to open this?" he said.

I nodded my head. "I'm ready now. I just had to tell you those things before we looked."

"Libby, I will never doubt what you tell me is true. I don't think you're silly. I know something happened to you when you were in the coma. Even when we can't explain things, it doesn't mean it isn't legitimate."

"Thank you, Daniel. I've been concerned about telling you. The experience was so astounding that I couldn't find the words to convey it to you. So tonight..."

"...this morning," he corrected.

"This morning I could wait no longer."

I reached over and took the little key on the red ribbon and held it tight in my hand.

"I'm scared, Daniel."

"Do you want me to do it?" he said tenderly.

"Yeah, I think I do."

He took the key and put it into the lock on the front of the box. He handled it as if it were a sacred artifact. It turned silently in the lock.

"It's open," I exclaimed to Daniel.

"Now, all I have to do is lift the lid," he said, looking directly into my eyes.

"I know," I replied. We need a drum roll or something," I said, smiling through my nervousness.

"I feel like I'm a tomb raider or something," he said, returning my smile.

Inside, on top of some papers, laid a letter with my name on it. He gently lifted it out of the box and handed it to me. It wasn't sealed, just tucked inside the back part. I slipped the flap out, took the letter out and unfolded it. I recognized it immediately as her handwriting. As she aged, her hand had become shaky, and affected her writing.

"*My Precious Elizabeth,*

"*It will soon be Christmas time. It was wonderful having you home with me over Thanksgiving. It's been a long time since I saw you happy. Daniel sure lit up your face. You're moving on and that is so good. I'm sorry I didn't tell you how sick I was when you was in. I just couldn't ruin your happy days. I've kept things from Daniel about what was happening with me, but I thought it would get better, but it just got worse. I feel like I need to get this down before I get too sick to rite. So I set down and rote things you shoulda knowed. If you're reading this, then I have gone on to be with Jesus."*

I wiped the tears from my eyes so I could see the words. Daniel reached over to the side table and handed me a tissue, and I continued reading.

"Daniel, I hope you will fergive me fer making you be the one to tell her about her mama. I just couldn't. I'm so sorry. I kept this on my heart fer her hole life but not fer me, fer her. I just couldn't have her feel bad growing up. I put you through so much and again. I'm sorry but there weren't no one else I could trust.

"In the bottom of this box you will find a gold locket. Your grandmother gave it to your father the day we picked you up. She said the day might come and we…we…"

"I can't make out that word. Can you?" I said, holding the letter up for Daniel to see.

"Let's see," he said, rereading the section I had just read. "I think she means would, instead of woud."

"You're right." I continued.

"woud want you to see it. Inside is a picture of your mother. Her name is Rose Ann Ross."

"Ross was her name. We have a name to go hunt.

46

"She died giving birth to you at age 17. Your birth certifcate is in the box. I arranged for you to have one after I got you. Since your daddy was your real daddy he filled in all the things they needed. The last I knowed about your grandmother she was in West Virginnie. I think the name of the place was Craggy Rock. Her name was either Rachel or Ruth. I'm sorry, years have kinda fogged my mind some. I never seen or spoke to the woman. If you want to find her, I don't have a problem with it. As you look at the picture of your mama you will see you look just like her."

"Oh, my goodness! You do look like her," Daniel said, holding the locket in his hand. "Here, look at this."

"I think the good Lord did that as a punishment to your daddy. Ever time he looked at you he was reminded of the sin he done with her. God forgives but sometime we have to pay the price. Your daddy loved you child. He never blamed you for nuthin and I didn't either. I loved you from the minet I layed eyes on you. I just have a feling that Daniel will ask you to marry him one day. He is a wonderful boy, Elizabeth, I hope you say yes. I just wish I could be there to see it happen, but I don't think I will. Just take care of each other and always be faithful to each other.

"You will find yer daddy's wedding band in there. I kinda wanted you to give it to Daniel to wear but it ain't no fancy thing. But it is yourn to do with what you want.

"Well my sweet child be good to Daniel and I hope you have some purty babys. Maybe God will let me see you from heaven.

"I will always love you

"Mama"

I picked up the birth certificate and read the words that had been printed on it.

"Elizabeth Ann Edwards, mother Rose Ann Ross. Two female children, one still born, and one alive. Mother died in childbirth, no other children. Attending doctor, Ad... Here, Daniel, you're a doctor, see if you can make out his signature."

"Oh, no, not the dreaded doctor's signature. Let me see." He took the document from me and held it so he could get a better view. "Actually it isn't as bad as some. It looks like Adam Waterhose."

We both started laughing and couldn't stop.

"I think we're both punchy. Look again it couldn't be Waterhose." I said, still laughing. "No wonder they died."

"Waterhouse, that's what it is, it's Waterhouse. I've never heard that last name before, either," Daniel said, still laughing about the other name.

"It also says you were born in Morgantown, West Virginia. That gives us an area to look in. Let's just pray it isn't a big county. This is really a great clue, though, because we have the doctor's name. All we have to do is look in the archives in that county and see where he had his office. Then we can do our snooping in that area.

"Daniel, do you think we will be able to find her on so little information?"

"It is God that will guide us. We will both search until there is no other place to look."

"Look Daniel, this is Daddy's ring that she was talking about." I held it up between my fingers. "She wanted you to wear it."

"Let me see," he said, taking it from me.

He slipped it on his finger to see if it fit. It fit perfectly.

"I know this was special to your mother, but I could never replace the one you gave me on our wedding day. I think we can do something special with it, though. If you would trust me with it, I would like to take it."

"Of course I would," I said, taking it from him to hold.

"This is the sum of your fears, my precious Libby. There was nothing here for you to worry about. Maybe this weekend we could start looking. I'll ask Chris to hold down the fort while were gone. What do you think of that?"

"I think you're the most precious gift God could give to me."

"Other than your life," Daniel said, pulling me close to him. He took the box from my lap and placed it on the night stand. "It's been a long, long night. How about snuggling with me, and maybe we could even a take a little nap."

"Are you sure napping is all you want to do?" I asked, sliding down under the covers close to him.

"I didn't think these words would ever escape my lips, but yes, my sweet wife, all I want to do right now is sleep beside you."

"Honeymoon's over, I guess," I said, fluffing my pillow under my head.

"Honeymoon's just resting, we have the whole day to stay in bed if we want to, it's Saturday."

It was only a few minutes until I heard his deep breathing. He still had his arm over me holding me close to him. This was the way he went to sleep every night. I'm sure if I had moved it would have awakened him, so I just laid still and let my mind wander over the past few hours.

I held Daddy's ring in my hand. I wondered what Daniel had in mind to do with it. I pressed it to my lips. Did he wear this ring the night I was conceived; this ring that was a token of eternal devotion. Could one be so easily pulled into adultery? I looked at my own ring, knowing in my heart that it would stay pure forever. I guess Mama felt that sure one time, too. Then the gold turned to brass, but the blood of Christ turned it back to gold. Mama had asked me to not hate him. If I hadn't taken my trip to heaven, maybe it would be harder to forgive. My angel mother took this orphaned little girl and raised her and made her believe she was a princess. The burden she must have carried on her small shoulders. What a price sin had paid, but at least the last half of their marriage was happy.

Now my thoughts have to go from the past to the present. I have an angry, bitter grandmother somewhere in West Virginia that I have to find. Wonder what she would think of this grown woman she handed so carelessly to another? Maybe she had mellowed over the years. Perhaps she has gotten saved by now. Maybe she would even be glad I have come to find her. I know our steps are ordered by the hand of God.

I loved these times when I could lie in Daniel's arms. He had become my protector, my lover, my best friend, and ordained by God to be mine. How could I be blessed twice with such love? I felt the arm Daniel had stretched over me relaxing as he went into a deeper sleep. I felt myself relaxing, slipping into dreamland with him.

Chapter Three

Daniel and I got the things from Mama's house that I had requested. Mandy and I got Jonathan's christening gown and bonnet washed and put away. Some day, I thought, if God gives me a child, I would like to have him or her to be dedicated to the Lord in this little outfit. A new week had come and almost gone. Daniel and I had planned the trip we would make to West Virginia. We had planned to go as soon as he got off work that day. He was hoping to be a little early, but we know how doctors' offices are. I had everything packed and ready to put into the car. We would stay overnight somewhere on the way. The weather forecasters said it was supposed to be a beautiful spring weekend, with the promise of sun with no rain. We had located Morgantown, but didn't see Craggy Rock anywhere. Daniel had mapped out the route he would take. It was up in the northern part of West Virginia, so it would take a few hours to get there. He said we would stop and ask people about the area we were looking for there.

I was so excited I could hardly contain myself. He called from the office and said he was on his way. Mandy had fixed us a small picnic supper that we could eat on the way. I felt like a kid at Christmas time. I was in the bathroom when he came home.

"Hello, anyone home?" he said, as he came into the bedroom.

"Here I am," I said, coming out of the bathroom.

"Umm, you smell so good," he said, planting a kiss on my lips.

"I just finished taking a shower and fixing my hair and makeup."

"Darn, just a few minutes earlier and we could have showered together," he said, pulling me closer.

"We don't have time for hanky panky. We have a trip to make."

"There's always time for hanky panky," he said, nuzzling my neck.

"Okay, I'm going to go take a shower. I think I need one right now," he said, moaning as he went.

By the time he got out of the shower I had already put our suitcases and picnic lunch in the car. I went up to the bedroom just as he was finishing.

"Umm...come here you smell so good," I said to him.

"Stay away from me. You had your chance," he said, holding me at arm's length.

"I bet you'll change your mind later."

"You're probably right," he said, pulling me in his arms for a long kiss.

"I have everything in the car ready to go," I said, leading the way down the stairs.

"If I don't miss my guess, you're awfully excited. It's good to see you so happy," he said as he followed me.

"You make me happy, Dr. Scott. You've helped me face a lot of fears. There is no fear in this only adventure."

"Maybe we'll find her this weekend maybe not," he said.

"Are you feeling lucky?" I asked him.

"Not today," he said, smiling at me.

"I didn't mean *that* kind of lucky. I meant like really lucky."

"Oh, you mean that kind of luck. Yeah, I feel lucky. I tell you something that's better than lucky, and that is being blessed. We've prayed about this, and I think God will answer, if not this weekend then we'll go again."

"I know we're blessed. Every day I have with you I'm blessed."

We were finally on the road at four o'clock. It was a beautiful afternoon. The time had changed, and the days were longer. Things were beginning to bloom and the leaves were putting out.

"Honey, I called about the mobile thing. They said we could order it. They said it will take a few weeks, but we get to pick out all the things we want in it. They said they have equipped several of them to be used in the field. I want you to help me and Chris pick out and design the thing. We've also found a federal connection that will subsidize part of the money because we are going to be using in it in Appalachia."

"What did Chris think about the idea?" I inquired.

"He was real excited. He was wondering how we would work out the schedule, since I will still be at the clinic. I told him we would figure out all the details later."

"Did you tell him I was going to be your nurse?" I said, smiling.

"Yeah, he couldn't believe his ears. He said he would rather have you in the office with him than in the other place. He said you actually belonged in the ICU area. That you were an excellent nurse."

"I didn't know he paid that much attention. We nurses felt so used sometimes."

"Believe me, sweetie, we noticed."

"He also said you need to come in for a checkup. You're long overdue."

"I'm doing great," I returned.

"But he just wants to be sure. You were terribly ill."

"Daniel, I was thinking, since the money is coming from the sale of mine and David's house, do you think we could dedicate the mobile in his memory?"

"Sure, but I don't think I could stand seeing his name on the side of it all the time. Can you understand that? I think I could go with a plaque or something."

"I'm sorry, Daniel. That was thoughtless of me. We don't have to do anything like that."

"Don't be sorry, after all, that's why we'll have one isn't it, because he died."

"What I was thinking is that we might go to community centers or churches and have someone preset the appointments. At least they could tell people we're in the area, and when. If we found some that were real sick we could send them to the local hospital for further testing."

"You've really thought this through, haven't you?"

"Yeah," I said smiling at him, "I've been working on it."

"I tell you what, you make the plans and then you can meet with me and Chris and we'll all go over it together."

"You mean you trust me enough to design this thing?"

"Why shouldn't I? You're a brilliant woman. You need a chance to show what you can do. I think you know exactly what you're doing."

"It makes me feel good that you trust me."

"I think you could order all the supplies and Chris and I could take care of ordering the medicine. We should be pretty well set up."

"I'm so excited about this, Daniel. Just think that you and I will be working together to make a difference to these people."

"I think some of the pharmaceutical companies might donate some of the medicine."

"That would be great," I exclaimed.

"You caught my dream didn't you?" he said, reaching for my hand.

"When you first mentioned me coming back here, I couldn't believe you were even asking me that question. I was kind of offended that you would want me to come back after all the years we fought to leave it."

"It was hard for you to understand that, wasn't it?"

"Very much so."

"Isn't it amazing how God puts things together?"

"I'm hungry. How about some of that food Mandy made?"

We traveled on for three hours and decided to spend the night at a hotel. We would finish our trip in the morning. Hotels were few and far between, so we decided to take the next one we came to, as long as it wasn't a flea

57

bag. Daniel spotted a Holiday Inn and pulled in. He went to register while I sat in the car. He was soon back with our key and we went to find our room.

"I got us a king size bed," he said, taking the suitcase out of the car trunk. "I don't know why I did. I think a twin would be sufficient. We don't get that far away from each other," he said, grinning at me. "But it's there in case we need it."

"I guess we could roll from side to side," I said, returning his smile.

The room seemed a little cramped with the king size bed, but was nice enough. We went to the restaurant that was in the hotel, and ate a late-night snack. After getting back into the room we undressed and climbed into the big bed. He turned the T.V. on and I cuddled up in his arms. Before I knew it, I was sound asleep. I woke up early in the morning with the T.V. blaring. Daniel was sound asleep; as usual, he was curled up close to me. I found the remote under the sheet and turned it off.

I eased myself out of bed to go to the bathroom and made my way back to the bed it the dark. I tried to quietly slip back under the cover so I wouldn't wake him. As I slipped under the cover, he reached for me and instinctively pulled me close to him.

"I love you," he whispered in a sleepy voice, as he drew me even closer.

"I love you, too," I whispered back to him.

David was the opposite of Daniel. He wanted all his space and couldn't stand to have arms or legs thrown over him. He loved to be cuddled, but not while he was sleeping. I loved feeling Daniel's closeness as I drifted off to sleep. I sighed deeply and drifted into a dreamless slumber.

We didn't have a wakeup call on purpose. Daniel had to be up and out very early in the morning to do his rounds at the hospital and to get to the clinic for regular hours. It was always good to sleep in for a while. We had a late breakfast at the hotel restaurant and hit the road. We were still a ways from Morgantown. The day was sunny and lovely but the air was still cold enough that we had to wear jackets.

We talked most of the way about the new medical mobile we were planning. Daniel told me he was planning to put a small surgical suite in the very back of the trailer, just in case there were some small procedures he could perform there. The more we talked, the more excited I became.

"You know you're going to have to get your license to practice in Virginia, don't you?" Daniel asked.

"Yeah, I've been thinking about that. I was wondering if I will have to take some classes to get caught up on procedures," I inquired.

"Honey, if there's anything you need to know I'll teach you," he said, smiling at me.

"Are you being condescending to me? I have flashbacks to my childhood and you always having to be the doctor."

SEARCHING FOR MY MOUNTAIN

"Would you like to be a doctor?" he implored.

"No thanks, when would we ever see each other? I'll settle for being your nurse."

"How prophetic our childhood was. Could we have ever dreamed it would be reality?"

With the conversation, it seemed no time until we were at the town limits of Morgantown. Daniel planned to stop at one of the older stores and ask one of the locals if they knew of a place called Craggy Rock. I was hoping our search would be profitable.

We saw a store not far from the city limits. I went in with Daniel so I could get a soft drink. The workers behind the counter seemed too young to remember anything very far back in history.

"Hi, we're looking for a place that is supposed to be in the area, it's called Craggy Rock. Would you happen to know where it is?"

"No, I don't think I have ever heard of it," the young girl said. "I haven't lived here long. Maybe somebody else could help you."

"Thank you, we'll check around town," Daniel said, taking his change from her.

"It's about time for lunch," I suggested. "Maybe we could look for one of those little family restaurants. Usually those are run by locals who would know the area."

60

SEARCHING FOR MY MOUNTAIN

We drove through town and spotted a little restaurant called 'The Blue Plate Special'. There were four or five cars in the lot. White ruffled curtains decorated the big plate glass window. The large rocking chairs that lined the porch looked very inviting. There was half of a whiskey barrel filled with the remains of last summer's flowers.

A strap of leather with bells on it hung on the door and announced our arrival as we entered. The waitress greeted us and had us follow her to a booth that was located in front of the big window. Each table had a small juke box sitting at the back of it, and for a quarter you had a choice of a variety of country songs.

"What can I get you two to drink?" she asked.

"Do you want tea?" Daniel asked, looking at me.

"Sure, tea would be fine," I returned.

"I'll be right back. Ya'll take ya time lookin'. The specials are on the inside sheet. The vegetables are right under the specials."

"Thank you." we said in unison as we looked at our menus.

She was back in just at few minutes. After sitting down our drinks, she was poised with pen in hand, ready to take our order.

The name "Susie" was printed in large black letters on her handmade name tag. Her hair seemed to have been bleached one time too many, and was pulled up in a ponytail on top of her head. The permed curls cascaded down over her forehead.

Her nails were short and painted a bright red. Faint smears of polish were here and there around her cuticles where she had tried unsuccessfully to remove the mistakes.

Her eyes were outlined with black, and her eye lids donned a brilliant blue eye shadow. Her cheeks had vivid red rouge apples painted on each one. The deep wrinkles that formed around her mouth and eyes seemed to belie the image of youth she tried so hard to convey. When she smiled, her whole face lit up, and softened the harshness of her makeup.

My mind wandered back to my teen years. Looking at Susie reminded of all the things I worked so hard to avoid. I could see the ruggedness of what life in the mountains could do. Now my vision was tempered with kindness on those that chose, or should I say, ended up living a life of poverty. Maybe at one time I did look with disdain on the mountain people. I guess I saw the hardness of their life, and wanted an easier one for myself and my children.

I observed a seemingly happy person, despite the difficulties that the mountains had delivered. Supposedly my grandmother didn't fair so well, if my dream or vision held any truth to it at all. The roughness became a dagger in her heart that slowly and surely killed her spirit.

I'm one of them, I thought. My heritage and my roots started right here in this quaint little town, or somewhere close by. I was jogged from my daydreaming by the return of Susie.

While she was pouring our tea, Daniel asked her about Craggy Rock.

"Excuse me, is it Susie?" he asked, looking at her name tag.

"Yep, that's me," she said proudly, looking down at her tag.

"Do you happen to know of a place around here called Craggy Rock?"

"Well now, that sounds familiar, but I just cain't seem to place it. We have all kinds of places around here stuck off in the back roads. Sometimes only the people that live there know what it is," she said, laughing, "Mama's been here a lot longer'n me. Let me go ask her."

She disappeared through the swinging door at the back of the restaurant. She came bumping back through with an older grey-haired lady in tow.

"Hello, my name is Judy Watson," she said, extending her plump little hand to Daniel. "Susie says you want to know wher' Craggy Rock is?" she asked in her mountain drawl.

"That's right; do you think you can help us?" Daniel asked.

Susie came with the food we had ordered and sat it on the table in front of us wielding the platter of food with expert hands.

I believe ther's a place down near a dairy farm that's called that. It aint' a very big place, but I'm sure it's the one you'll be lookin' fer."

"Would you mind giving us directions there?" Daniel asked.

"I'll go write 'em down fer ya," she said. Not waiting for a reply, she waddled back through the swinging doors.

Daniel and I ate our food. Susie made several stops by our table to make sure we were well taken care of. Toward the end of our dinner, Judy came to our table with a sheet of paper in her hand.

"Well, if I 'member right here's the directions. It's about six or seven mile down Blackbird road. You'll find that road at the end of town. Take a left at the stop light and go as far as ya can, and it'll stop, there you'll have to go right or left. Go left till ya come to a sign sayin' 'Till Farm Road'. Turn left again and about three mile down the road you'll see a little community there and that will be Craggy Rock. There might be a store or two, but not much more'n that."

"Thank you so much," Daniel said politely, taking the paper from her extended hand.

"What ya goin' there fer?" she asked.

I was taken aback a little by the directness of her question.

"We're going to look for a lady who used to run a tavern there many years ago."

"What's her name? I used to go to the taverns some when I was younger."

"Her name is Rachel Ross, and we aren't sure what the name of the tavern is."

"There weren't all that many taverns around here, so I could name ya off a few. Maybe that would help."

"Sure," Daniel said.

"Well, there was Billy's Place, and there was The Thirsty Traveler, and Rooster Rest. They's all I recollect bein' around here. Oh, and I do 'member one more, The Waterin' Hole."

"Which one was the closest to Craggy Rock?" Daniel asked.

"I believe that would have been Rooster Rest. That was the one the coal miners used to flock to all the time. I used to go there some, and it was a rough place."

"Did you happen to know the owner's name?" I asked.

"Well, like I said, I didn't go there much, and I was much younger then. If my thinkin's right she was one rough lookin' tough talkin' lady. I guess you'd have to be to put up with them rough miners," she said with a chuckle. "But I don't 'member no name."

"Thank you, it's really nice of you to try to help us."

"I hope ya find who ya lookin' fer," she said, shaking our hands.

The jangling of the bells said goodbye the same way it said hello, as we exited the restaurant.

When I got in the car I studied the directions she offered to us.

"We go straight down the street to find Black what Road?" he asked, pulling out into the street.

"Blackbird Road," I returned. After that, you turn left at the stop light and go as far as you can and then you will have to turn right or left, go left until ya come to Till Farm Road. Turn left again." I said, smiling at the way she had written the directions.

"I just need to remember to always go left and I'll always be right," he said, laughing.

After turning at the stop light in town we drove several miles and came to the dead end intersection.

"I go left, correct?"

"Correct."

"How far is it until we see this 'Till Farm road'?" he inquired.

"It doesn't say, it just says 'go until you find it.'"

"That could be several hours, or five minutes," he said.

"I have a feeling it won't be very long," I said.

"The country is really pretty back in here, isn't it? Look up there at the garden on the hillside," I said, pointing out the landscape.

To harvest, all you would have to do is let the vegetables roll down to you," he observed. "How in the world did they get a plow up there?"

"Daniel, look, we're coming to another intersection. Maybe it's Till Farm Road," I said, squinting, trying to see the road sign.

Sure enough, as we rolled toward the sign I saw the lettering and it was Till Farm Road.

"I know, another left," Daniel said, as he turned the wheel. "So according to what's her name this should take us to Craggy Rock?"

"Yeah, Judy. That was her name. And that's what it says. We should go right to it."

"Or left to it," Daniel said, still laughing about the directions.

About four miles down the road we could see a few more houses than usual. I felt that we were coming into a little settlement. I saw a store coming into view.

"I think this could be it, Daniel. It seems to have a store."

Daniel pulled up beside the gas pump. We both got out and went inside together. There was an elderly man behind the counter.

"Howdy, folks, what can I do you fer?" he said with a big toothless grin.

"I'd like to get some gas," Daniel said.

"Would ya like it filled up?" he asked, heading outside to the car. "And do ya need the oil checked?"

"Just fill her up and you don't have to check the oil," Daniel said.

I got Daniel and me a Coke out of the machine and proceeded down the aisle to get a candy bar for us. I took my items to the counter to purchase. By the time I had collected them, the old man had returned to the store. There was an old fashioned cash register sitting on the counter. He slowly and methodically totaled the sale.

"Will this be all?" he asked.

"We need to ask you some questions about this place."

"Fire ahead," he said, smiling at us. He turned his head slightly toward us and cupped his hand behind his ear so he could hear better.

"What is the name of this place?" I asked, as he most intently listened.

"Blake Mountain," he returned."

SEARCHING FOR MY MOUNTAIN

I felt my heart sink a little.

"Could you tell us if you've heard of a place called Craggy Rock?" Daniel asked.

"Yes, indeedy," he said proudly. "You would miss it if you didn't know what ya were lookin' fer." He gave a little chuckle as he continued. "It ain't no town. It's just a spot in the road. You won't find no signs. It's just what people around here call it cause of the rocks near the coal mines. They used to do some strip minin' up there. It left the rocks bare, so they called it Craggy Rock."

"How far is it from here?" Daniel asked the little old man.

He rubbed his bearded chin while he was thinking. "It's about six miles, as the crow flies," he said.

"How far is it in people miles?" Daniel asked.

"Well, they's a workin' on the bridge that goes over Fox Creek, so it's closed. That used to be a short cut through there. But they ain't one now. So you just have to go without the short cut, and that'll take you about eight miles, 'cause you have to circle back. I could take you another way but I'm sure you'd get lost, so I won't tell that way."

"Does this road circle back, or do I have to take a turn off?"

"You'll turn off this road after about five miles. The road you want to take is Mine Shaft Road. There'll be a sign fer it, but you have to keep yer eyes open. It's right after you cross over this big hill.   You'll come right up on it, real quick."

"Will there be any place where we might ask for directions once we get there?" I asked.

"If I 'member right there'll be a store like mine, and maybe a small rester'nt where ya can eat a bite."

"Maybe we better get some more snack food in case we can't find this place. We might get pretty hungry before we find a restaurant."

We wandered through the store, picking up various things we might like to munch on. Once we made our purchase, we walked back to the car to continue our journey.

"I didn't think he would ever get the directions out. He took us all the way by the short cut to tell us it didn't work," I said, smiling at Daniel.

"One thing we know we don't want to do is go over Fox Creek," Daniel said.

"Definitely not Fox Creek," I added, smiling at him.

We drove over several hills, thinking each one may have the illusive Mine Shaft Road on the other side. Daniel had tuned in some music on the radio and we were enjoying that. The scenery was beautiful and changed at every turn in the road. There were tiny houses with monster TV dishes in the yards. It seemed in this poverty stricken area that these expensive satellite receivers were a necessity of sorts. There wasn't much to brighten their dreary lives, I guess. Maybe the TV shows they watched

70

carried them to a place away from their pain and misery, and the sacrifice seemed somehow worth it.

"A penny for your thoughts," Daniel said, reaching over to squeeze my hand.

"I was just thinking about these people. What they must go through living in poverty and squalor. What kind of dreams do they have; what hope and aspirations do they have? What do the young people do with their lives?" I answered.

"Those are worth more than a penny," he returned. "To answer your question, they have dreams just like we did, and do. Some are very wise and intelligent. Their dialect and dress sometimes makes us think they aren't. We were cut from the same cloth, sweetheart."

"I know, but some get out of poverty, and some don't. What makes the difference?"

"That's a million dollar question. If I had the answer, I would be a *very* rich man."

"Maybe they don't see themselves as being in poverty," I stated.

"I never knew what poverty was. We always had whatever we wanted. Maybe God blessed us because he used Mom and Dad to help supply the needs of the community. They were so freehearted with everyone, and in turn, the customers responded by being faithful to pay back what was extended to them."

"We grew up in a wonderful place, didn't we, Daniel?"

SEARCHING FOR MY MOUNTAIN

"As I get older and wiser I can see more clearly what I had growing up. I never was made to feel superior to anyone. Mom and Dad never acted like that to anyone. I thought everyone grew up with maids until I was older."

"You never made me feel like you had more than I did."

"Maybe it was because I didn't think I did."

"Did I ever tell you how we came to have Charlotte and Mandy?"

"No, I don't think you ever did."

"Mom told me this after I was grown. Charlotte was a young woman in her twenties when she got pregnant out of wedlock and her family disowned her. She came by the store one day, hungry and with no place to go. Mama got to questioning her and finally learned the story. She took Charlotte home with her that day and gave her a place to live and took care of her while she had her baby. Unfortunately she lost her baby at birth. Mom told her she could continue to live with her as long as she wanted to. All that she wanted in return was someone to help her care for the household while she ran the store. A deal was made, and Charlotte became one of our family. She was like a mother to me."

"How did Mandy come into the picture?"

"That's a sad story, too. Her mom and dad were killed in a house fire. A neighbor happened by and rescued Mandy from the house but couldn't save her mom and dad. There weren't any relatives in the area to take her in. The story was circulated around the store. Mom just couldn't stand the thought of no one wanting this girl. She talked it over with Dad and Charlotte about her coming to live with us. She was about twelve at the time. So after the family meeting it was decided that Mandy would become part of our family, too. Mandy became the child Charlotte lost. She mothered her and cared for her. I don't know who needed who more, Charlotte or Mandy."

"And I thought you were just spoiled," I said, shaking my head.

"That just goes to show what happens when you assume things. What we did was give two precious people a life. They always had the opportunity to go or stay. We never held them at our place. But they loved us, and we them. Charlotte and Mandy wielded a heavy hand where I was concerned. I didn't get by with anything. I respected their authority, and if I hadn't, Mom would have set me straight."

"We were doomed from the start, Daniel. My mother took this little stranger in to rear as her own. And your mom and dad took people in to give a home and job to. We inherited this need to help these people. God knew when he took us away that he would bring us back. We were destined to come back for these wonderful people. I wouldn't doubt that our moms prayed us back here."

"You were a stubborn little thing. God almost had to knock you in the head to get you back here."

"You forget, he did knock me in the head," I said, laughing.

"You're right, how could I forget that?"

"When God lifted the shades from my eyes so I could see, it saddened my heart. Mama died because she was embarrassed to tell you she was bleeding. There are hundreds of people just like her that are ashamed of the things happening to them. We need to educate them some way. I'm hoping the medic mobile will help them."

"I love you more all the time. I never thought that would be possible, but it is. I can't believe it sometimes how God not only gave me my first love, but also placed in her the same dreams I have," he said tenderly.

We had just crested another hill and were headed down the other side when it dawned on me we had just passed Mine Shaft Road.

"There it was, Daniel; it's the road we're looking for," I exclaimed.

"I'll find a place to turn around and we'll head back," he said, slowing the car.

He got the car headed back up the hill to the turn off. It seemed such an odd place to have a road. It looks like the builder could have placed it at the bottom of the hill instead of the top," I said.

"You'll turn right from this direction," I reminded him.

"No kidding, I wouldn't have known that if you hadn't told me," he said, teasing me.

He slowed the car to exit onto Mine Shaft Road.

"I guess from here on out we don't know exactly what we'll find," he said.

"What do you think the chances are of finding her on our first try?" I said wistfully.

"I don't know," he said, taking my hand in his. "But if we don't this time, we'll keep looking."

We had driven about three miles when we saw a gas station looming on the horizon. It looks like we'll get to investigate some more.

The area we entered into was a little more populated than the area we came from. The houses were rundown and shabby looking.

We entered the station and approached the counter where and older lady was sitting.

"Hiedy," she said in a warm and friendly voice. "What can I do fer ya?"

"We're looking for a place called Craggy Rock. Do you happen to know where that is?"

"Yer standin' in it, or what's left of it," she said with a chuckle.

"We're looking for a lady that used to live here. Her name is Rachel Ross. She used to run a tavern. There was a lady in Morgantown that said there used to be a tavern here called Rooster Roost," I said.

"I think ya mean Rooster Rest," she said, smiling at Daniel.

"What ya want to know fer?" she asked, squinting at us, as if to size us up. "Is she in trouble?"

"No, I'm a relative of hers and would like to see her," I answered.

"I reckon the onliest ones that would want to see her would be kin. I don't reckon she has many of 'em left. Ya sure she ain't in no trouble?"

"I'm sure."

"I don't want to get her riled up at me. Ya don't want to be on the wrong side of Rachel. I figgered she done run off all the people that would of keered fer her. She was a hard woman, she was. Didn't have a kind word fer nobody. I guess I'm one.

"Rachel ruled that old tavern with an iron hand. She's the onliest one that ever run that place."

"How well did you know her?" I inquired.

"Ya sure ya ain't the FBI or sumthin'? she asked again.

"No, honestly I am her relative," I said, smiling at her.

She seemed to relax as she talked. "I figgered she done run off anybody that was a kin to her."

"And you don't know where she lives?" I asked.

"I know 'xactly wher' she lives. She wanders in sometimes, but she don't say much. She's gettin' purty old, and cain't get around much, but you still don't want to get her riled up. She can cut ya sixty ways to Sunday, and spit on ya as she walks away," she said, still keeping a keen eye on me.

"I ain't never been to her place. Only one person I know of goes to see her. She lives way back in the woods somewher' purty close.

"She used to have a friend named Hazel Jones that lived up in Spring Holler."

"How do we find her?" Daniel asked.

"I might need to give her a holler and see if she's still close to her. Let me go in the back room and see if I can find her phone number in the phone book. I'll be back, Ya'll make yerselves at home," she said, leaving the room.

"Daniel, we're getting so close," I said excitedly.

"Don't get your hopes up too high. Okay?"

"Okay. I'll try not to, but it's going to be hard to do."

It seemed like we waited forever before she returned.

"Well, I talked to her and she agreed to meet ya. She said she don't know if she will be able to help ya or not."

"Where do we meet her?" Daniel inquired.

"Well, ya just keep goin' down this road your on and she will be out at her mail box. You won't be able to miss her. She said to tell ya she'll have a yeller dress on."

"Straight down the road, yellow dress," Daniel said to make sure he had the right directions.

"Yep, right straight down the road."

"Thank you so much," we said as we left her quaint store.

"I love it," Daniel said, chuckling. "The directions she gave are so unique. Keep your eye out for the little lady in a yellow dress."

We drove a short distance down the road, and true to her word, there stood a small-framed lady dressed in yellow standing at - you guessed it, the mail box. Daniel slowed to a stop where she was standing.

"Hello," I said after rolling down my window.

"Hiedy, are ya'll the ones I'm supposed to meet?"

"I guess we are. We're looking for Rachel Ross."

"Don't nobody look fer Rachel. Who might ya be?"

"Well, it's a long story, but I'm her granddaughter."

"She ain't never mentioned no grandchild."

"I know, I only found out myself a short while ago."

"Would ya'll like to come in and visit awhile?"

"Sure," Daniel said.

"Come and park your car down by the house," she said, motioning in that direction.

Daniel slowly pulled our car down the little dusty drive to her house. By the time we had parked and had emerged, she was waiting for us on the front porch.

"You children come on in."

Daniel and I made our way into her humble living room. Everything was neat and in order. She was such a gracious little lady.

"Y'all can call me 'Hazel'. What can I call you?"

"Excuse us for not introducing ourselves earlier. I'm Daniel Scott and this is my wife, Elizabeth," he said as we extended our hands to her.

"Can I offer ya'll a glass of tea or sumpthin'?"

"No, we're fine," Daniel and I answered in unison.

"Well, tell me about how ya come to know Rachel."

"I just learned from my mother on her death bed that the one I called 'Mama' all my life was not my real mother. My mother died giving birth to me. She was Rachel Ross's daughter."

"I knowed Rachel when Rose died. She was real quiet about the whole thing. At first she told me Rose had a baby and they both died during the birth, but she never mentioned there was another baby. Not at first, anyway."

"I understand she had twins and one died and one lived. I'm the one that lived (of course). My father, the one that fathered us girls, was a miner here and I guess he got drunk at the tavern one night and that's when he got with her daughter, Rose."

"I didn't know for a long time that Rose was in the family way. It was when she died that Rachel came to me and wanted to know if I had any burial land. I thought for a long time that Rose had gone to live with an aunt somewhere in Norf Ca'liner. Then I found out she was here all the time. Rachel kept her shut up in the back room. It was then my heart broke fer that little girl."

"How did you find out about how she was treated?"

"Stories get around, and I think the midwife was the one what told the real story. I did find out right before she was due that she was pregnant. I knowed she didn't have no doctor. I kept tellin' her to let Dr. Adam check her, but I think she was just ashamed and said the midwife could take care of her. So I let it drop. You know, you just don't go wher' ya ain't invited. Ya just got to respect other people's privacy. Anyway, she said that Rose was doin' good, and was real healthy.

"The story goes that she was in labor fer about three or four days runnin'. I think the midwife just up and left when things went bad. She didn't say a word, just left that little girl in a real bad way. Rachel finally got Dr. Adam to come. His last name was Water sumthin'. We just called him Dr. Adam. When he got there, one baby was

80

already born and dead, and you was stuck sideways in her. Rose was already dead when he got there. It was told she bled to death. So all Dr. Adam could do was get you out. He took a knife of sorts and cut you out of her stomach. Yer a miracle, that's all I can say, is yer a miracle. Like I said, I never saw you or even knowed you were in the world."

"She didn't say anything to you about a second child."

"No, she just said she needed to bury her daughter and grandchild."

"You never saw her other child?"

"No."

"Wher' did you go?" she asked, looking at me quizzically.

"My father came and took me to his home, and his wife became my mother."

"Rachel don't know you're lookin' fer her?" she inquired.

"No, I just found out not too long ago what her name was. So this hunt to West Virginia came out of some records my mother left me in a box."

"I don't 'xactly know how to tell her. What do you say to someone?"

"Well, at least she knows I didn't die. Does she have a phone?"

81

"No, she don't."

"Well, can you take me to her?"

"Maybe I need to go see her first and tell her about ever'thing."

"I don't have much time. Daniel and I have to get back to Virginia tomorrow."

"If you could just give me today to go see her, and prepare her, that would be good. You know she ain't in real good health. I would hate to kill her with the surprise."

"I wouldn't want to kill her either, but I don't think it would. My husband is a doctor and would be ready to take care of her if something happened."

"What do ya want her fer? If ya just want to find her and ya gonna be mean to her, then I'm not sure it would be good."

"Hazel, why in the world would I be mean to her, she's the only blood family I have. I just want to get to know her."

"But because she give you away you just might jump on her fer that."

"Hazel, I can't begin to understand what happened when I was born. I know without a doubt I was raised exactly where God wanted me to be. I don't know why things happen the way they do, but I was raised to love God and to love others. My father made a terrible mistake by getting Rachel's daughter pregnant. But he lived the remainder of his life going to church and raising a Godly family. I guess he paid for his mistake over and over throughout the years."

"I didn't go up to the tavern much. I kept Rose Anne fer Rachel when she was little. Rose was three when her daddy died. He was killed in a drunken brawl at the tavern. She could never remember him.

"After his death Rachel changed. She was hard, with her words and her life. She could cut ya to the bone by her words if ya done her wrong. She loved little Rose, but had a hard time showin' it. She was a good-looking little girl. She had shiny brown hair, jest like yers. Beautiful, she was. After Rose got on up in age, Rachel kept a hard hand on her and she wasn't seen much. I think all she did was go to school and come home and stay in the back room. As she got a little older, her mama let her wait on customers some."

"So you knew my mother well?"

"Oh, yes, she was a lovely little girl. She was as sweet as she could be. Her smile would light up the whole room when she walked in. Always quite, never loud, she just evidently got caught up in drinking one night, and you were conceived. I think she was a lonely little thing."

"I guess that's why she was attracted to my father, because she was so lonely. She wasn't a bad girl, was she?"

"A bad girl? Heavens, no. Not Rose Anne. She just wanted some love and affection and got it in the wrong place. How old was ya when yer Daddy took ya home?"

"Not more than two or three weeks old."

"I knowed it couldn't 'a' been too long. I don't think she coulda kept ya a secret for long. Course like I said, I didn't go up there to the tavern, but ya must 'a' been a good baby or she couldn't a kept the tavern open."

"I think that's why she was so desperate to get rid of me," I mused.

"Your mama must 'a' been an angel to take you and raise you, bein' you was the other woman's baby."

"Yes, she was an angel. I didn't know how much so until recently. The reason she kept the secret was that she was afraid I would feel like I was only here because of an accident. She also said she didn't want me to be called a… a bastard," I said hesitantly.

"No one's here because of an accident. You were created by the Master. He doesn't accidentally create something, He creates everything on purpose."

"You're a wise woman, Hazel," Daniel said.

"Do you two have children?" she asked, smiling at first one, then the other.

"No, but we're working on it. We hope to soon," Daniel replied.

"What line of work do ya'll do?" Hazel asked.

"As Elizabeth said, I'm a doctor, and she's a nurse."

I saw her eyes light up with the information Daniel had given her.

"I don't think I been this close to a real doctor before."

"You don't have a doctor?" Daniel asked.

"No, I've been blessed with good health, just an ache or two here or there. I wish I could say the same thing fer Rachel. She looks awful bad." A cloud of sadness crossed over her face as she thought of her friend.

"How did you two become friends. Was it just because you kept Rose Anne for her?"

"Nah, me and Rachel go back a ways. We were friends in school. We always were doin' things together. Those were happy days fer Rachel. She weren't always hard and bitter then. It was only after she married that she became so mean with people. I married right after she did, so we just kinda went our separate ways. I would see her around and we would talk about gettin' together, but she was busy with the tavern and my husband didn't want nuthin' to do with that place. Church people didn't hang around places like that. But me and Rachel stayed friends. I think she knew why I didn't come around."

"Where is your husband?" I asked.

"He died about twelve years ago. He had a heat stroke out in the hay field. He didn't live to say goodbye," she said wistfully.

"I'm sorry."

"I didn't remarry. So Rachel and I kinda took up a closer friendship after our husbands died. Her little Rose filled up a lot of lonely hours fer me."

85

"Do you see her often?"

"Neither of us drive, so it's been a while since I seen her. It's been about a month since I seen her last, I reckon."

"Does she live close by?"

"Just down the road around the corner. There used to be a road goin' down to her house, but it's kinda growed up now with weeds and stuff. There's a little creek ya have to cross over with a foot bridge."

"Maybe we could go with you and wait in the car while you talk to her."

"Well, maybe, I just don't know."

"We won't go in unless you say it's okay," Daniel offered.

"Okay, let me get my coat. It's kinda chilly today."

We waited while she gathered her things and made our way out to the car. My stomach was churning with the prospect of seeing this woman. I didn't know what to feel or how to act. I tried to rehearse what I would say, but the words wouldn't come. Daniel reached over and squeezed my hand.

"You won't have to do this by yourself. I'll be right by your side," he quietly said only for my ears to hear.

"Right around this curve you will see a mail box. That's the lane to Rachel's house. I don't know if you dare

86

drive there. You might could make it to the spot where we cross over the bridge. You could wait fer me there.

Daniel drove slowly over the rutted driveway. It was a long drive. By the time we reached the place where the foot bridge was, we could no longer see the mail box.

Across a little stream on a small rise was the house of my grandmother. It was a depilated shack that had a porch going completely across the front. There was some kind of seat that reminded me of one from a school bus. Three or four large dogs ran down to the bank of the water, growling and barking at our car. I saw a large-framed woman standing in the open doorway. Hazel was proceeding across the bridge when I heard her call out to Rachel.

"It's just me, Hazel. I came to see how you're doin'. Call yer dogs."

I heard her call out several names, and the dogs came running to her. Hazel slowly made her way up the worn path to the porch. Rachel never moved toward or away from her approaching friend. Our car was partially hidden by the overgrowth of brush and trees. I'm not sure if she saw the car, but she didn't seem to.

Daniel pulled me over to him and kissed me.

"How do you feel?" he asked, looking tenderly into my eyes.

"I feel nauseated and nervous."

"I won't let her bite you," he said, smiling at me.

"I know, it's just that this is all so unnerving." I returned his smile weakly.

It had been such a long time and still no Hazel. We listened to the radio and talked about one thing after the other. She had been in there an hour, but it seemed so much longer.

"I wonder if she has told her yet. I wonder if she's refusing to see me. Then what will I do?" I asked nervously.

"Sweetheart, you're driving yourself nuts. Just don't think about it."

"That's easy to say, but hard to do," I said, taking a deep breath.

We waited about ten more minutes before we saw Hazel cross the bridge. I got out and approached her as she was walking toward me.

"Well, she will see ya."

"What did she say?"

"It's hard to tell how she feels, she don't show much emotion. The reason I was so long, I just couldn't get up my nerve. I finally just blurted it out. She said to come on over. She was going to chain the dogs."

Daniel, Hazel and I trudged across the bridge and up the hill toward the house. Rachel stood on the porch.

"Ya'll come on up and have a seat," she said.

We sat down on a make-shift bench. They were indeed old bus seats. Daniel sat beside me, and Hazel sat on the far end in an old rocker. Rachel took her place directly beside mine and Daniel's. She didn't fit the description I had been given of her. She didn't look or act mean at all.

"My name is Elizabeth Anne, and this is my husband, Daniel Scott," I said, putting my hand out to shake hers.

She hesitantly took it and gave me a stiff little shake.

"So you're Rose Anne's baby," she said, clearing her throat.

"Yeah, that's what they told me. I only found out a few weeks ago."

"What do ya want from me?" Rachel said, still not looking at me.

"I don't want anything in particular. I just wanted to get to know you. You're all I have left, and I felt like I needed to find out more about the family I never knew."

"You ain't missed nuthin'. What ya see is what ya get."

She finally lifted her head and looked at me. I saw an empty shell of a woman. Her face was lined with heavy wrinkles.

Ya look just like her, ya know. She had hair the same color as yers. It's been a long time since I 'llowed myself to think back. Is yer daddy dead?"

"Yes, he died a few years ago, and my mother died..." I hesitated for a moment realizing that my real mother was her daughter. "My mother died a few weeks ago. It was then that I found out she wasn't my real mother, but your daughter, Rose, was my mother."

"My daughter Rose was yer mother. For a few brief moments she was yer mother."

"She will never cease being my mother. Time doesn't alter the fact that she is who she is. I had a wonderful woman that took me and raised me as her own, but she isn't the one that gave me life, she just sustained my life. Rose would have been so happy to know this lady. She couldn't have loved me more if she had given birth to me."

"Do you want me to feel guilty for givin' you away?"

"No, I didn't come here to make you feel bad. I came here to get to know the grandmother I've never known. I would never come to make you feel bad. You did what you had to do. God made it all turn out right. I had my father. He changed after I was born. At least that's what Mama said. She said she wouldn't take me if he wouldn't quit drinking. So, true to his word, he started going to church and never drank again. He was a good man, he just ..."

"I know what he did, and it cost me my girl's life." I could hear the pain in her voice.

"I know it won't bring Rose back, but the reason my dad would drink so badly was because he lost a little baby boy. He just couldn't get past the pain. He tried to run from it, but it haunted him, I guess."

"My Rose wasn't no angel. I guess they both found what they was a lookin' fer, but couldn't see the price they would have to pay."

"Do you think we could have some kind of relationship? Maybe I could come and see you, and we could get to know each other."

"Maybe, I ain't gonna promise. I don't know much about havin' family. Maybe that's why God took all of 'em away. God might take you away if ya get too close."

"Well God and I will work that out," I said, smiling at her tentatively.

"I'm tired now; if ya don't mind, I think I need to lie down," she said, getting slowly to her feet.

I guess that was the signal to say goodbye.

"Daniel and I will be in the area until tomorrow. Can I come back and see you one more time before I leave?"

"You can do whatever ya want to. It don't matter none to me."

"What should I call you?"

"I guess whatever ya want to."

"Well, I guess I'll call you 'Grandma Rachel'. Would that be okay?"

"If that's what ya want."

I went to her and gave her a hug. She was stiff and awkward as I put my arms around her.

"You better go now," she mumbled.

"I'll come back tomorrow and you can tell me about my mother," I called to her as she ambled into her house.

Daniel, Hazel and I made our way back down the dirt path we had come in on. I wasn't sure what I was feeling at the moment. I don't think victory would be the word I'm looking for, maybe relief, perhaps pity.

"She seemed fairly mellow," Daniel said, patting my knee.

"I'm glad ya'll let me go in first, I think it holp some," Hazel added from the back seat.

"Well, I guess we need to go find a place to stay for the night," Daniel said.

"There's a place out on the main road. It's a small place, but it clean. I know the family that runs it. If I'm not mistaken the name of it is called the 'Midnight Serenade'," she said.

"Umm, sounds like a good place to me," Daniel said, winking at me then pursing his lips.

I punched him in the ribs and laughed at him. We slowed to turn into Hazel's driveway.

"Ya'll can just let me out at the mailbox. I can walk."

"I'm already turning now. I insist on taking you to your door," Daniel said.

He got out of the car and opened her door for her.

"You're such a nice boy. I ain't never had nobody open my door fer me," she said, grinning up at Daniel with her toothless little grin.

He walked her all the way to her front door, and when he left her, she was still grinning.

"You made her day," I said to him as he got back in the car.

"I think I'm ready to take you to the 'Moonlight Serenade', and let you make my day," he said, leaning over to give me a kiss.

"You think you can handle me?" I said, smiling at him.

"I think I'd like to try, Mrs. Scott."

I always liked it when he teased with me.

"What did you think about your grandmother?"

"I'm not sure. Do you think she liked me?"

"I know she did. What's not to like? She said you looked just like Rose. That's why I know she liked you."

"She felt so stiff when I tried to hug her."

"She probably hasn't been hugged in a long time, and doesn't know what to do."

"What will we talk about tomorrow?"

"Maybe she will tell you about your relatives. You might want to find out about health issues to see what runs in the family. You may be susceptible to diabetes or something. You never know."

"Yes, Dr. Scott."

"I think these curves are making me nauseated. I'm feeling a little sick to my stomach."

"Probably from all the excitement. We might need to get something to eat. When we find our hotel we'll look for a restaurant."

It didn't seem to take as long getting back to the main road as it did coming in. We followed Hazel's directions and came right to the hotel. There was a small café across the street. We registered, got our key and walked to dinner. The people there were very friendly, just like all the other places we'd been to on our trip. We ordered the Saturday special.

We talked throughout dinner about our trip thus far. It seemed our steps had been predestined. It wasn't as hard as I thought it might be to find Rachel. Having a name and place sure did help the hunt. There were a lot of things I needed, or I should say wanted, to ask my grandmother. Would she be willing to answer? I thought to myself.

After dinner I was still a little nauseated. Daniel suggested that I take an Alka-Seltzer, and proceeded to try to find some at the little drug store down the street. He asked me to rest in the car while he got something to ease my nausea.

Our hotel room was small and smelled musty. The scent of the carpet suggested that some heavy smokers had visited the room prior to us.

Daniel found a glass in the bathroom and brought the bubbling concoction to me where I was stretched out on the bed. I hated the taste of Alka-Seltzer, and shivered as I drank the last of it.

"This may help if I can keep it down. I think I'm going to go take a quick shower," I said, grabbing my train case and pajamas.

"I'll go after you, or we could shower together," he hinted.

"I don't think we would both fit, it's so small in there."

"Okay, I'll be waiting for you."

I got the water as hot as I could stand it and let it cascade down over my tired body. I let my mind wander back over the day. I still was trying to sort through my feelings of the past few hours. Before the day began I wondered what would happen when I saw her. I wondered how I would feel knowing she was my grandmother; looking at her for the first time. I also pondered about what she thought of me. I felt sorry for her in one way. She must have been a very lonely lady. Would tomorrow bring more unanswered questions or would I come away satisfied? For now I needed to get out of the shower and let Daniel have his turn.

"I was about to send a search party to hunt you," he said, smiling at me as I rounded the corner to the bedroom.

I put on my pajamas and snuggled down under the cover to wait for Daniel. I must have fallen asleep, because when I woke up it was dark and Daniel was asleep beside me. So much for the Midnight Serenade Hotel, I thought, smiling to myself. I would make it up to him tomorrow.

Tomorrow, Lord, go before me and prepare my way; I pray things will go well for both my grandmother and me.

Chapter Four

Daniel and I slept late. There was a soft rain falling on the hotel roof and the room was darkened by the drawn curtains.

I felt his kisses on my neck as I was waking up.

"Good morning, my princess," he said, still nuzzling my neck.

"Good morning, yourself," I returned. "Sorry I fell asleep last night. I was trying to stay awake for you."

"Yeah, I hurried through my shower, just thinking about you waiting for me. And you were sound asleep," he said in mock disappointment.

"I'm sorry. I'm not a very good wife am I?" I said, turning over to face him.

"I guess I'll have to trade you in for a new one," he teased.

"Please, Dr. Daniel, I promise not to fail again."

"Okay, one last chance, but if you fail me again you're a goner," he said, pulling me to him.

SEARCHING FOR MY MOUNTAIN

It didn't take me long to respond to his arduous ovations. Our departure could wait awhile longer, I thought, as I snuggled even closer to him.

At breakfast I felt the nagging nausea return. I hoped I wasn't coming down with something. I managed to eat breakfast and it seemed to settle everything down.

We made plans for our last day there. We calculated that we could head back home late in the afternoon and still get home at a decent hour. It was almost eleven by the time we finished breakfast. We figured Grandma Rachel would be up and about by the time arrived. We headed back down the winding roads we traveled the day before. The twist and turns in the highway seemed to bring back the reoccurring nausea.

"You look a little green, are you okay?"

"I've never had problems with car sickness before, but the curves sure do seem to bother me today," I said, holding my hand on my stomach."

Tell me if you need to stop. I'm a little concerned. I remember the last time we went through with the nausea thing. Is your head hurting?" he asked, with concern rising in his voice.

"No, no headache this time, just this queasiness. Eating seemed to help though."

"I think there are some crackers in the basket that Mandy packed. Let me stop the car and see. I know

98

crackers help morning…morning sickness," he said more slowly.

We suddenly looked at each other with full realization of what might be wrong. My breath caught with excitement.

"Do you think we could be pregnant?" he asked, grinning from ear to ear. "When did you have your last period?" he questioned.

"Well, let me think," I said, my mind trying to calculate the last time I had a period. "Let me see, if I'm right, I *am* late, but I do this sometimes. But I don't usually have the nausea, but it could be the curves in the road."

"And you had it last night and this morning."

"Yeah, but let's not get our hopes up yet. Maybe it's just the curvy roads."

He pulled over to the side of the road and stopped the car. He went to the trunk and retrieved the crackers and a soda we had in the cooler.

"Libby, let me get excited," he said, as he opened my car door. "Just think, you could be carrying our baby right now."

"I just don't want you to get your hopes up and me not be pregnant."

We instinctively put our hands over my stomach. We just couldn't keep the smiles from our faces. He pulled me to him and kissed me.

"Tomorrow you're coming to my office and we are going to find out for sure."

"But for right now, we need to go see my grandmother."

It was around 12:30 when we arrived back at her little cottage. The dogs were still on the loose running up and down the creek bank barking at us. I could see Grandma Rachel standing on the porch as we exited the car.

"Come on boys, get back under the porch," she hollered at the dogs. They obeyed like loyal soldiers.

When they were safely under the porch, Daniel and I started over the little foot bridge.

"Come on up to the house, they ain't gonna bite. They jest like to bark."

I could have sworn I saw a little smile at the corner of her mouth.

There was still a slight drizzle in the air. Fog shrouded the surrounding mountain. I felt in my heart of hearts that today would be a good day.

She stood at the porch railing as we walked up the dirt path. I saw a toilet peeping out from behind the house, so I assumed she didn't have a bathroom. We walked up the rickety old porch steps. Daniel had a firm grip around my waist.

"Be careful with your step; we don't want you to have any accidents," he said softly, smiling at me. The first trimester is the trickiest."

"Daniel, we don't know yet."

"But I don't want you hurt either."

"You two come on in the house. It's kinda' chilly out today. I've got a fire a goin' in the stove," she said, leading the way into her little home.

When I walked in, it reminded me of Bessie's house the night we went up for her viewing. It hit me fully as we entered the room. I took off my sweater and held it in my lap. She motioned for Daniel and me to sit on the sofa. Thank God, it was at the far corner, away from the stove.

She was the first to break the awkward silence.

"I didn't think I would ever see ya again. I told ya goodbye the day ya left and that was that."

"Did you ever wonder about me, Grandma Rachel?"

"Oh, I wondered about ya all my life. I couldn't let myself get too caught up in it though. It hurt too bad. Fer when I would think of you, I would think of my little Rose."

"I felt yer Daddy would love ya, he seemed like a decent man."

"I wanted to tell you my mother named me after your daughter. She asked my daddy what my mother's

101

name was and she said it was only right that I carried on a small part of her. I don't know if I could have done the same if I were in her shoes."

"Ya musta' had a good mama to do that."

"I had a wonderful mother. You see what happened was, Mama and Daddy had a little boy. He was just a few months old. Daddy ran away from his pain to West Virginia and Mama was left behind. He buried his pain in a bottle, and Mama took hers to the Lord. I was born out of his loneliness and pain. He found solace in Rose. I can't apologize for him, but I can say he turned out to be a good man."

"Rose was lonely, too. I guess I kept too tight a grip on 'er. I was afraid she would turn out wild, and I kept her holed up in the back of the tavern, and it happened anyway. She was a beautiful girl. I guess she took after her daddy. He was a looker, he was. He had a tough time with the bottle and it ended up killing 'im,"

"I'm so sorry you lost so much. It must have been very painful."

"I tried to push it all to the back of my mind, but it didn't stay there."

"I wish I could have been there for you over the years, but as it was I didn't know who you were."

"I was cursed all my life. I was meant to be lonely and sad. It came because I operated the tavern. My grandmother told me no good would ever come of me because I put the bottle to people's mouth. I guess she was right. All I ever knowed was pain and suffering."

"It doesn't have to be like that always," I assured her.

"It's too late fer me. I'm gonna' die here a lonely old woman."

"You don't have to stay a lonely person. There's got to be some joy that will come your way."

"I had some joy yesterdey when you came to see me. You look so much like Rose; it took me aback how much. I thought fer a minute I was seein' a ghost."

"No, I'm for real, and if you'll let me, I would like to be the granddaughter to you that I am. Your giving me away didn't change the fact that I'm your family."

"You're the only family I have. I don't have another livin' soul to call mine," she said, wiping at her face.

I could tell she was embarrassed at the unbidden tears that were falling down her cheeks.

"I fixed ya'll a little bite of dinner if ya want some."

She got up and headed to the kitchen. Daniel and I followed her. She had three plates set at the small dining table in her kitchen. She had fried some chicken, and I could see it piled in a platter on the counter. She made her way around the kitchen, putting things into dishes. She had green beans and mashed potatoes, and some corn-on-the-cob. I could see a pan of cornbread sitting on the back of the stove.

"It's so nice of you to fix lunch for Elizabeth and me. We really appreciate it. Elizabeth was just commenting on the fact food might settle her stomach."

"Are ya with child, Elizabeth?" she asked pointedly.

"Well," I said smiling, "I don't know. I have to have a checkup when I get back home and I'll know for sure. Daniel sure hopes so."

"Make sure ya have a doctor. I learned my lesson with Rose," she said sadly.

"I'll see to that," Daniel interjected.

"Did I 'member ya sayin' you were a doctor?"

"Yes, that's right. Elizabeth and I grew up together in Virginia. Then she went away to become a nurse and I went away to become a doctor and here we are at your doorstep."

"You listen to him," she said, looking at me.

"I will," I said, smiling at him.

"Is there anything I can help you do?" I asked as she piddled around the kitchen.

"No, I have everything under control," she returned.

"Are you sure? I really don't mind."

"Well, if ya really want to you can put the food on the table. That would help."

"I can help, too," Daniel said.

"No, you just stay put. We'll wait on you." She returned.

We had an enjoyable dinner. I tried not to think about how clean her cooking was. I figured God would take care of everything and not let me get sick.

It was getting late and by the time we finished dinner and I helped her with the dishes it was time to leave.

"Grandma, it's time for us to go, but we'll be back to see you real soon."

She reached out to me for the first time. I felt her give a little this time when I placed my arms around her. We had a lot of time to make up and we wouldn't do it in one day. We bade her goodbye and made our way down the footbridge to our car. She had even given Daniel a hug goodbye.

We turned around, and were headed back to the world we came from. But I wouldn't return the same. My grandmother had become an integral part of our lives now. We would make sure we didn't forget her. She gave Daniel and me Hazel's phone number and said if we ever needed her, Hazel would get a message to her.

Chapter Five

I was at Daniel's office early on Monday morning to visit with Dr. Roger Stanley, the new gynecologist. I don't know who was more excited, Daniel or me. I had continued the nausea and still hadn't seen a period. My appointment was for 10:00 o'clock. I arrived a little early so I could see Daniel before I went in.

"Honey, we should have the test results soon. I'd be willing to bet money that you are pregnant, if I was a better, that is," Daniel said, patting my tummy.

"Would you like to go have this pelvic exam?" I asked him.

"No, I don't think I can help you there, but I'll pray for you while you're in there."

"You don't mind my being examined?" I teased him.

"No, not from a doctor's point of view, but I would mind if it was Chris, since we are such good friends, and he wants to marry you if I die. Yeah, I would mind if Chris was doing a pelvic."

"You silly man, what if Chris was the only one here?"

"I guess I would just have to get over it."

"Well, it's time for me to go. I'll see you in just a few minutes." He kissed me and told me to go find out about our baby.

Dr. Stanley was both very young and professional. If he was ill at ease because Daniel was my husband, it didn't come across in the exam.

"Well it feels like you're pregnant. Your uterus seems to be a little larger than the time frame you've given me. Could it possible you're further along than you think?"

"That's one thing I'm quite sure of. Daniel and I married Valentine's Day and he's the only man in my life."

"I didn't realize you had just gotten married. I didn't mean to imply that..."

"I was just teasing you."

"Is there a problem with the early enlargement?"

"No problem, it could and I want to stress *could* mean that you're carrying more than one."

I took a sharp intake of air.

"You're kidding, aren't you?"

"No, I wouldn't kid you about this."

After finishing a pap test, he told me to get dressed and he would meet me back in his office. When I arrived, Daniel was already there.

"Have you told him anything?" I asked Dr. Stanley.

"No, I was waiting for you to join us. You tell him," he said, smiling at me.

"They're going to do a urine test to make sure, but he really thinks we are going to have a baby."

"And what else?" Dr Stanley said, raising his eyebrows at me.

"Is something wrong?" Daniel asked, suddenly concerned.

"I want you to tell him," I said, looking at Dr. Stanley.

"Will *someone* tell me?"

"Like I was telling her, I'm not totally sure, but from my exam, her uterus seems to be a little larger than it should be for the time frame we're talking about. Think, Daniel..." he said, smiling.

"Oh, my God! Twins, it could be twins?" He grabbed my hand and his mouth fell open. For once the good doctor was speechless.

"We'll know more when we can hear heartbeats. But I just want you to know it still could be just one. What am I doing? I'm sitting here telling this to a doctor that does this every day," he said, laughing at himself.

"Are you okay? Is she okay?" He redirected his question to Dr. Stanley.

"She is in perfect health. She needs to get vitamins and rest; you know how to take care of her, doctor," he said, smiling at Daniel.

"I can't believe this, two…" Daniel exclaimed.

Dr. Stanley got up from his chair and came around to where we were sitting.

"I've got another patient I have to see. You can use my office to regroup. You know, Daniel, I didn't say twins, what I said was it could be more than one." He patted Daniel on the back and walked out of the room, not waiting for his last comment to hit Daniel and me.

"I just letting the word 'twins' sink in, but what if it were three?"

"Oh, man, was I ever thrown for a loop. I was all ready for the pregnant thing, but I didn't let myself think multiples," Daniel said in shocked disbelief.

"We've got to remember, he said 'could be,' not 'is.'"

"Yeah, we need to hang onto that thought. What if it is? Are you okay with that?" Daniel asked me tenderly.

"I was barren for so long, whatever God gives me, I will be happy with. I have a wonderful husband that will take care of me," I said, leaning over to kiss him.

We heard a light tap on the door. His nurse poked her head into the room.

"Dr. Scott, you have a patient that is ready to be seen in room five."

"I'll be right there," he said to her. "I've got to go, baby, but stick around and we'll talk in just a minute. I hate to leave you," he said, pulling me into his arms. He kissed me warmly and tenderly.

The nurse had left the door ajar and Chris entered the room catching us off guard.

"That's not allowed during office hours. I've told him over and over not to hit on our patients," he said, laughing at Daniel.

"Hey, Chris, it's good to see you," I said, giving him a hug.

"Since you're here, Mrs. Scott, I need to see you in my office. You're long overdue."

"I hope those words don't ring true," Daniel and I said, laughing.

"What did I say?" Chris asked.

"'Long overdue,' I hope those aren't prophetic words. You tell him, Daniel."

"We just found out you're going to be an uncle, Chris."

"No way! Congratulations. When will you be due?"

"Sorry, I forgot to tell you that important information. We got sidetracked on another issue," Dr. Stanley said, entering the room.

We all said in unison, "When?"

"If what Elizabeth tells me is true, and I don't doubt that, and I emphasize, *don't doubt that*, it should be the end of December."

"Wow!" came from all of us again in overlapping trio.

"Chris, are you an integral part of this pregnancy? You seem so excited about Daniel's baby," Dr. Stanley said.

"We've promised Chris he can be an uncle," Daniel explained.

"You see, Chris was going to marry her, but he didn't know she was single and by the time he found out I had already asked her to marry me. So we've kind of adopted him into our family."

"You guys confuse me," he said, shaking his head.

"He also saved my life. I would have died if the good doctor hadn't of done emergency surgery on me. I had a blood clot on my brain," I said, smiling at Chris.

"Chris, there's something else we need to tell you about her pregnancy," Daniel said seriously.

"Is there a problem? After all, I'm your doctor, too, and I need all of the information."

111

"It's possible that we will have more than one."

"No way! Boy, you must be fertile," he said, smiling at me. "No kidding, I do need to see you even more now," Chris said, his voice changing to a more serious tone.

"Will you have time for me now?"

"Yeah, I'll fit you in. I'll tell Karen to put you in a room.

"Okay, I'll see you guys later."

"Daniel, I want to see you as soon as you finish with your patient," Chris called out.

"Meet me and Elizabeth in my office."

"Okay, I'll see ya."

Karen told me to follow her.

"You need to come in here and give a urine sample."

"Okay."

As soon as I was finished, she came and took me to the exam room to wait for Chris.

"I'm going to go get your chart and put it outside for the doctor," she said, exiting the room.

Chris wasn't too far behind her.

"How you doin'?" he asked, looking at my chart.

"I've been doing great. I just have this nausea that seems to have an explanation. Pregnancy does that to some women."

"You're glowing, I think that's what they say happens when you're pregnant. You seem very happy and content."

"I couldn't be happier. I'm just flabbergasted about the possibility of having more than one baby."

He took his light and looked into both eyes.

"Have you had any dizziness, double vision, anything I should be aware of?"

"Nope, I'm feeling wonderful."

He felt of the scar where he did the surgery.

"I'm happy for you and Daniel. God not only spared your life but he has given you another one to bring into the world."

"I will never be able to thank you enough for what you did for me," I said, giving him a hug.

"Just take care of yourself. Come, let's go into my office. Daniel is supposed to meet us there."

We had no sooner seated ourselves when Daniel came in.

"How is she doing?" Daniel asked.

113

"There is one small thing I want to discuss with the both of you," he said, looking from one to the other of us.

"You sound so serious Chris," Daniel said.

"It's about the baby, I don't want to burst your bubble right now, but I do foresee a possible problem."

"And...?" Daniel questioned.

"Knowing what I know about you, and having done your surgery, I don't think you will be able to have a vaginal delivery. I think it will put too much pressure on the area of the surgery. There is a tremendous amount of pressure during the pushing stage of delivery, and I don't want to take a chance on you rupturing something."

"But you said I had healed so well," I stated.

"You have, but there is a big question mark about a lot of pressure. You may deliver fine, but I would strongly suggest C-section."

"Wow, I didn't think about that. But I can see where you're coming from," Daniel interjected.

"I just don't want you to get to the end and have to have emergency surgery. You two are very special to me, and you know I wouldn't tell you something that wasn't true."

"I know, I didn't even think about my surgery in the context of having a baby."

"C-sections aren't all that bad, your recovery is a little slower, but all in all, I think you would do great."

114

"Thanks for the advice, we will proceed with caution," I told Chris.

"Multiple babies, how about that. I'm going to have to rest up; it looks like I'm going to have a busy Christmas," he said, smiling at Daniel and me.

"We're going to go have lunch and digest all our news. She didn't keep a lot of her breakfast down, so I want to make sure she has an early lunch," Daniel said protectively.

"Keep in touch with me, Elizabeth. I'll talk to Roger Stanley and tell him my concerns. He's a great doctor to be so young. He will take excellent care of you," he said, hugging me. "Don't worry about what I just told you. But I felt as your doctor I needed to. See you guys later."

Since getting back from West Virginia, Daniel and I had been very busy. The medical mobile had come in from the factory and we were so excited at its arrival. I had ordered all the supplies except the medicine and Daniel had ordered that. Daniel and I would take turns with the other doctors going on the mountain trips. They seemed more than glad share the adventures. Daniel and I would have first shot, since it was our dream. We would go the first and third Thursdays in every month. We had already designated places to go. They would be divided among church fellowship halls and community centers. Daniel's and my first two assignments were ready to work.

There was a nurse with the health department that was more than willing to go ahead and spread the word that we would be coming. Her name was Sharon Light and she was a real top-notch, caring worker. She said she knew just the way to get the word out. She was going to set up radio spots, announcements on Sundays, and mailbox flyers.

She would have the people there, signed in and ready to be seen when we arrived. She was allotted a small staff from the health department, so she had all the help she needed. The next Thursday was d-day. I couldn't wait to get started.

The nausea was abating and my appetite was ferocious. I could tell that my waistband was getting snugger. Daniel was pleased with the fact that I could eat again, and keep it down. He was so protective of me, and I cherished every moment of it. His mom and dad were beside themselves with joy concerning the baby or babies. We hesitated telling them about the possibility of twins, but decided to let them in on all aspects of their future grandchild. Grandmother Scott had broadcast the information all over the county by that time. My next visit with Roger, he said we should be able to hear the heartbeat. Daniel had been listening everyday with his stethoscope and tried to hear them himself, but hadn't yet. He said he was going to bring home a special listening device that Roger had so we might be able to hear it. We had a nightly ritual of listening for the heartbeat. He thought he heard it one night, but decided it was gas. I was having so much fun watching Daniel watch me.

Early in the week that we would take our first trek into the hills and hollows of Virginia, Daniel, Chris and I met at the medic mobile and had prayer over it; asking God to bless all that came into its doors. When we went to our little dedication, Daniel had a surprise waiting for me. He had had the manufacturer place a small plaque on the entry door in memory of Dr. David Mason. I was moved to tears that it came voluntarily from Daniel and not my pushing for it. He *had* remembered my asking him. I thought he'd likely forgotten it altogether.

I was anxious to go over and do another recheck of everything, but Daniel put his foot down. Between him and Mandy, I was going to have a rough time getting to do stuff, especially if it was strenuous at all. I might have to get Chris to talk to him about chilling out some. He was concerned about my traveling with him, but I assured him it was perfectly normal to work during pregnancy. Some women work right up until they deliver, but I was sure that wouldn't be the case with me. One more day and we would have our first trip.

Chapter Six

The next day would be the beginning of our mission. I doubted I would be able to sleep. I just had finished my shower when Daniel came up from downstairs. He went back to make sure he had locked the door to the medic mobile. He had brought it home from work so we could start from here. Chris came over and had dinner with us. I guess we were like kids with a new toy. Chris had really caught hold of our dream for the mountain mission. He was chomping at the bit for his turn. We had a rotating staff to go with the doctors, so I only had to travel with Daniel.

"Do you think you will be able to sleep tonight?" Daniel said.

"I hope so. I'm so excited, I feel like it's my first day of school," I returned.

"I know what can make you rest," he said teasingly.

"But you don't want me overly tired, doctor. You yourself told me not to overdo it."

"It's been proven that it is very healthy for pregnant women to have sex."

"I know it's very healthy for the husband of the pregnant woman to have sex," I said mockingly.

118

"Oh, I just about forgot." He raced out of the room and down the stairs. "I'll be back in a minute," he called over his shoulder.

I turned the cover down on the bed and was just crawling in when Daniel hurried back into the room.

"Look what I have," he said, holding up a small black case.

"Oh no, doctor, what are you going to do?" I said in mock horror.

"This, my little princess, is what I'm going to hear my little baby's heartbeat with. Or should I say *try* to hear my little baby's heartbeat."

I pulled my top up so he could get to my tummy and he put the sensitive device in place. I lay in absolute stillness while he moved it over my stomach. There was a volume button that would amplify the sound, if he found it.

"There it is. I can hear it, sweetheart, I can hear it. Listen..." he said, turning up the sound.

I heard the swishing of the little heart. Tears began to flow at the beautiful sound we heard. Daniel leaned down and kissed my stomach twice where he heard the beating.

"That was from Mommy and Daddy," he said.

"Did you just hear one?" I questioned.

"I guess I need to keep checking, don't I?" he said, as he continued to listen.

"What do you want Mama, do you want me to hear two or three?"

"I'm not even going to answer that. I'll be happy with whatever you find."

"Okay, here goes." He continued to move the device up and down my stomach.

"Oh, my goodness, I hear another one, here, down at the bottom." His eyes were wide with amazement.

"Don't tease me, Daniel, not about this."

"I'm not, sweetheart, listen." He turned up the volume and there was the soft swishing sound of another baby. He took an ink pen and marked the first sound and did the same with the second one. He went back and forth, from one to the other listening to the sweet beats of their hearts.

"God is making them as we speak. He's knitting their little bones together," I commented.

"This is awesome, honey, we found it together. It's like hunting treasure. I've got to call Roger."

He reached for the bedside phone and dialed his private number. I could only hear one side of the conversation, of course.

"Hey Roger, this is Daniel. We've got two."

"Yeah, I definitely heard two."

"Three, I don't think so. I just heard two. Do what? Okay, thanks for letting me use this. I can't tell you how good it sounds. Okay, I'll see you day after tomorrow. I will be out of the office tomorrow. Do you need me to drop this by? Will do, goodbye."

"He said for you to turn over on your side. We might find three."

"This isn't an Easter egg hunt," I said, turning on first one side, then the other."

"Well, I guess I only hear two," he said disappointedly.

"Only hear two!" I exclaimed. "That's quite enough, don't you think?"

"I was kind of excited about three."

"But you're not the one carrying them," I said, laughing at his remark.

"Can I listen again?" he pleaded. "Just once more?"

"Sure," I said, "but you know you're taking away from daddy time. I have to try to get some sleep."

"I tell you what I think I'll listen more tomorrow," he said, grinning at me.

"What did Roger say about getting that thing back?"

"He said for me to keep it, he had another one at the office, and mentioned that I might need it on our trip. That's one thing we forgot to put in."

Daniel reached over on his side of the bed and turned out the lights. We snuggled close together under the cover. He caressed my stomach lightly.

"Libby, we heard the heartbeats. I'm one happy man, and I'm about to be just a little bit happier. What better way to celebrate than by making love to their mama?"

"You can say some of the most unusually romantic things, and this is one of them."

Later, as I was lying in Daniel's arms, the full impact of what had transpired really hit me. We were going to have two babies. How incredible that was. I placed my hand over Daniel's, the one that was resting on my stomach; I wondered what his thoughts were as he drifted off to sleep. My excitement was ebbing, and finally I could feel myself drifting off to where Daniel had already gone.

The clock alarm jarred me as it sounded its wake-up call.

"Daniel, are you awake?" I mumbled.

"Umm…"

"I guess that's a yes," I said.

"Are you going to shower first or am I?"

"I will let you catch a little extra sleep. I'll wake you when I get out of the shower."

"Okay," I mumbled.

I drifted in and out of consciousness. It seemed like he took an awfully short shower, I thought as he gently shook me.

"Time to get up, princess. Our day is awaiting."

I threw the covers off and made my way into the bathroom. Morning showers are more for waking up than getting clean, I thought to myself.

It didn't take long for my shower. Daniel was ready and waiting in the kitchen when I came down.

"Don't we look cute? This is the first time I've seen you in your nurse's uniform. You look awfully sexy. Come here and let the doctor give the nurse a good morning kiss.

"I hope the patients don't think you're as sexy as I do."

"Daniel, Daniel, Daniel, we have to get on the road," I said, smiling up at him.

"We're going to work together, can you believe it?"

"It's kind of neat, huh?" I returned.

"How about some breakfast?" he asked, handing me a cup of coffee. He knew exactly how I liked it and had it perfect that morning.

"Too early, I'll just have coffee, thanks. I'll eat later in the morning. I'll throw up for sure if I eat now."

"You'll eat later, promise?" he said, intently listening for my response.

"I promise I will, but how about you?" I asked him.

"We'll stop at Hardee's and get something later."

"Okay, then let's get going."

We traveled for about forty-five minutes before coming to a Hardee's. Daniel went in and got a couple of sausage biscuits and some coffee to go. We were almost there, so we decided it would be a good time to stop and regroup.

"How are you feeling now?" he asked.

"I feel good. I'm not having any nausea at all. The little guys seem to be doing okay today," I answered.

"Little guys, wow, it still hasn't sunk in. We're going to have two little ones. What will we name them?"

"I haven't got that far. I'm still trying to get used to the thought of carrying two."

"Does the thought of a C-section scare you?"

"No, I've seen them before. I think I can get a spinal and actually be awake for the delivery. I want to see them when they are born."

"Are you sure about that?" he quizzed me.

"Yeah, I am right now. Why, do you think it isn't a good idea?"

"It's not a bad idea; I just want you to be sure. It does cause some residual back pain sometimes."

"I'll take my chances, just to see them born, and plus, I don't want them to have any extra sedation."

"It'll be done real fast, so they won't get much, if any."

"I guess we can do some research. I still might try for a vaginal birth."

"You know what Chris said, honey; it could be bad for you. I couldn't take another time like I had at Christmas, and neither could you."

From what our directions said, that must be our rendezvous place. I could see the church steeple rising above the ridge in the road. I was anxious to see what the day would bring.

Sharon said she would be here waiting on us. From all the information I had received from her, we would have about fifteen patients to see that day. I knew that we would just have to wait and see how it all would play out.

We pulled into the graveled church parking lot, undid our seatbelts and stood to stretch our legs.

"Honey, can we pray?" Daniel said, hugging me.

"Please," I returned.

"Our Dear Heavenly Father, bless our endeavors, give me wisdom as we see these patients. Bless Libby's and my babies today." I heard a catch in his voice as he continued. "Take care of them and keep them safe. Help us to be a blessing to the people that pass this way today, amen."

"Amen," I echoed.

We heard a light tap on the side door. We opened it to a smiling Sharon.

"Hi, I'm Sharon," she said, looking up at us.

"Come in," Daniel said, motioning for her to come into the trailer.

"I'm Dr. Scott and this is my wife and nurse assistant, Elizabeth," he said, extending his hand to shake hers. I followed suit.

"I've been looking forward to this day for a long time. Everything has come together so smoothly," she said, grinning from ear to ear.

"It's nice meeting you, too," I said.

"Are you all ready to go? We already have people here. So far we don't have any cancellations from anyone. I have an assistant inside and she has already done the preliminaries on those who are here, like temperature, blood pressure, and the history.

"I have them coming pretty steady until four. Our fifteen patients have turned into thirty. But barring any unforeseen problems, we should be through by 5:00."

"I like a take-charge woman," Daniel said smiling at her.

"Was that a complement?" Sharon asked.

"It was definitely a complement. You don't know what inefficiency can do to a doctor's day."

"Actually I do. My husband is a doctor also." She winced. "I've kept supper warm many evenings because of that one thing."

Daniel nodded. "Then I don't have to tell you."

"Tell me how this setup is going to work?" she said, waving her arm to the back of the trailer.

"Follow me. This first room is where we will do intake. I will talk to them a little before I do an exam."

"What is at the end of the hall?" she asked curiously.

"This is a miniature operating suite. We can take care of minor surgical procedures here. I'm really proud of this area. It was given to us by the State of Virginia, as a grant of sorts. They offered, and we took it. We have a doctor on staff that has more connections than you could imagine. His name is Dr. Chris Thomas. You will really like him when he comes."

"Well, I guess I'll go get your first patient. His name is Jake Sowers. He's seventy-five, and says he doesn't have any problems," she said, smiling at Daniel. "He said he only came along with his wife, Ida, because she needs to see a doctor, and she says she coming so he can see the doctor."

"Well, this is going to interesting," Daniel said, shaking his head.

Sharon left us and went to get the Sowerses.

"Do you want me to stay up front while you interview them? You probably want some privacy."

"Good idea, when I'm ready, I'll call you. Go put your feet up," he said, giving me one last kiss.

Daniel had the door open for them. Both were feeble and had to be assisted up the steps. Daniel seated them in two chairs across from him.

"Hi, my name is Dr. Scott, what's yours," he said, shaking hands with each of them.

"My name is Jake Sowers, and this is my wife, Ida," he said.

"What can I do for you today?" Daniel said, looking at the fresh chart.

"He is... she is..." they said in unison.

I saw a little smile on Daniel's lips as I watched him from the front of the trailer.

"How about I give you both a check up?" Daniel said, smiling at the sweet little couple.

"How about my wife taking you into the exam room and I will be in, in just a minute?"

I took my cue from Daniel, and came and stood by him.

"This is my wife and nurse, Elizabeth. She will take very good care of you. If you will follow her, she will show you where to go."

I took Ida by the arm and led her down the hall.

"Jake and I will compare hunting stories until you get back."

I knew by the smile on Jake's face that Daniel had hit his hot button.

"You ever hunt, Dr. Scott," I heard him ask Daniel as we made our exit.

"Ida, I'm going to ask you to put this gown on so Dr. Scott can listen to your lungs and heart."

"Are ya sure? There ain't nuthin' wrong with me 'cept my ole joints hurt. See, the reason I come was fer Jake. He ain't been feelin' so good. I figered since ya'll was a comin', it would be good to get him to the doctor."

"Do you want me to help you into the gown? It can be kind of hard to close in the back."

"If ya don't mind."

"I get a bit swimmy-headed. Not ever' day, but sometimes I jest go stumblin', she said, laughing at herself. I go right over on my head sometimes."

I opened the door to signal to Daniel that she was ready.

"Do you want me to stay or go?" I asked Daniel.

"Stay, please," he said.

I stood out of his way, and watched as he gently and modestly examined Ida.

"Ida, do you check your breasts for lumps?"

"Well, Dr Scott, I don't have any."

"Ida, you've got to have breast," he said, trying hard not to laugh.

"Well, I did at one time. They's now not much there."

"Do you mind if I check you to see if you have any lumps?"

"I think I would know if there was one, but ya can look."

Daniel checked her for lumps and felt around on her stomach.

"How 'm I doin', doc?"

"You're doing great. Sit up and let me look in your eyes and ears."

He continued to give Ida a once-over. This was the first time I had ever seen Daniel with a patient. I was overcome with love for him. God had given me such a wonderful man as a husband.

"Your blood pressure is high. Did anyone ever tell you that?"

"I ain't been to no doctor to see."

"You've never been to a doctor," he asked in amazement.

"Well, there's one that would come to the house when the babies was born. But we always just doctored ourselves with herbs and stuff."

"Do you know what I mean when I say 'high blood pressure'?"

"Yeah, I know."

"When your blood pressure is high you can have a stroke, or heart attack. So what we need to do is get it to come down, and one way is by medicine. Then you will have to adjust your diet."

"We only have one kind o' food. It's the kind I always eat."

"It's the salt that you're going to have to cut out, or down, anyway."

"I do like the salt shaker," she said, smiling at Daniel. "But food tastes so bad without it."

"What kind of meat do you eat?"

"Mostly pig, you know, we kill 'em ever' fall. I can it and salt cure it. I can all my vegetables. I make my own bread. So I don't know rightly what you want me not to eat."

"Okay, let's do this, don't add extra salt at the table and cut back on some of the pork you eat. I'll give you some pills to take until I come back again and we'll see if it gets better."

"I'll try."

"That's all I can ask. You have some cataracts on your eyes," he said, shining a light in them. "You really need to have them removed. I bet you could see a lot better."

"I thought that was sumpthin' old people lived with."

"You don't have to live with them. It isn't painful to have them removed."

"Have you had them, too, Dr. Scott?" she inquired.

132

"No," he replied.

"Then how do ya know?"

"Well, Ida you got me there. I just read somewhere that it didn't hurt. It might be uncomfortable, but not painful."

"You can get dressed now, and I will give Jake the once-over, okay?" he said, shaking her head.

"I need for you to draw a little blood to get some tests done for Ida. I've written on her papers what I want ordered. Okay?" he said as we left the room.

"Yeah, I can do that."

"After that, she can get dressed, and then we can let Jake have his turn."

As Daniel started to leave the room, Ida called him back.

"Dr. Scott, Jake probably won't tell ya this but..." she hesitated shyly and continued in a hushed voice.

"He's been a bleedin' down there fer a while."

"Would that be his urine or his bowels."

"It's his pee. He can't hardly go sometimes and the pain gets bad."

"Thanks for telling me. I'll check it out for you. Okay?"

"Thank ya." she said, smiling at him.

Ida and Jake changed places.

"Elizabeth, Jake is going to have his prostate checked, so have him take everything off."

"Ever'thing?" he questioned as we made our way to the exam table.

"Yes, I'm afraid it has to be everything, so he can get *everything* checked."

"But I wasn't the one with the problem, it was Ida."

I almost laughed out loud at his comment.

"Here is the gown, do you think you could get it on by yourself, or do you need help?"

"Well, I'll do the best I can, then what I cain't get done, I'll let you do. Ain't nobody ever seed me without clothes on."

"Dr. Scott does these every day, and I promise he will respect your privacy."

"If'n I have to, I guess I can."

"Okay, I'll be right outside the door, just call me when you need me."

My heart went out to them. They were so embarrassed to have anyone look at them. But Daniel seemed to handle it so well. I could tell that he was going to win over these mountain people.

I was about to go in and check on him when he called for me.

"You can come in," I heard him say.

I entered to find him sitting on the table with the sheet wrapped tightly around him. His clothing was piled on the chair in the corner.

"I'll go get Dr. Scott," I told him.

Daniel stopped me before we entered the room.

"While I check his prostrate you can stay outside. I'm sure he'd be embarrassed with you in the room. It'll be hard enough with me. But I want you in there until then."

"Okay, but do you want me to go in now or later?"

"Come in with me now."

"How are you doing?" Daniel asked him.

"I'm a little bit cold right now."

Daniel checked his eyes and ears, and listened to his lungs and heart.

"You have a strong heart, and your lungs sound good. Do you smoke?"

"I smoke a pipe. That's all I ever smoked."

"If you will lie back on the table, I'll feel around on your stomach a little bit."

He swiveled around and I pulled the extension out at the end for him to put his feet on. He was a short little man and barely needed it. As Daniel examined him, I saw him wince with pain.

"Does that hurt when I push there?"

"That hurts purty powerful right there," he responded.

Daniel was pushing down near his bladder area, and into his side.

"Do you have any problems urinating?"

"Is that like peeing?"

"Yes, it's the same thing."

"I do pretty much all the time."

"Have you noticed any blood?"

"Well, now that you mention it, sometimes when I empty the slop jar I see something that might be blood. We use it at night so we don't have to go to the outhouse."

"How long have you noticed it?"

"Well, let me think, it seems about five or six months, off and on. I thought it would go away, and I didn't have no way to the doctor, so when they mentioned you was a comin' by, I wanted to get Ida looked at. She's been kinda stumbly lately."

"I'm going to ask my pretty little wife to step out and I'm going to check your prostate."

"What is the prostrate?"

"The prostate is what produces semen when you ejaculate."

"Oh, that's what does that?"

"Yep, that what it does, and sometimes it can become enlarged. This is caused by infection, and sometimes a cyst or a blockage. It can cause burning, flu-like symptoms, bleeding; it can affect your sleep, and may make your legs become restless at night."

"But what if you don't do it?"

"That could be some of the problem. Men need to 'do it', to help the prostate stay flushed."

"Do you do it, Jake?" Daniel asked without cracking a smile.

"I'll tell ya in private," he whispered to Daniel.

"I think that's my cue to leave. I'll go check on Ida," I said, smiling at Daniel.

I waited outside the door for Daniel to call me back in.

"Elizabeth, can you get some blood work on Jake?" And also I need for him to give us a specimen."

"Okay, will do."

When the tests were done, the two of them were seated back where they started. I would walk them back over to the church and bring someone else over, I thought. If all of them took this long I couldn't see how we could possibly be done by 5:00.

"Well, Ida, I'm going to give you some medicine for your high blood pressure. I have written exactly how you're supposed to take it. Don't miss any doses. When you come back to me, I'll give you some more. You won't have to buy it. And Jake, I'm going to give you a prescription for an antibiotic for your prostate. There was an enlargement there, and it could just be an infection. Remember what we talked about. When you come back to see me, we'll do a recheck and see if it's better."

"Okay, we'll be back."

I walked them back to the church. When they left, Ida gave me a hug and thanked me for all I had done.

"You just follow what Dr. Scott said to do and we'll see you in about two weeks."

I told Sharon's assistant, Lori to make them an appointment for our next visit, and to make sure they would be picked up.

The day was a long and arduous one. We didn't finish until almost seven o'clock. By the time we reached home and did all the paperwork, it would be past midnight. We had stopped long enough for lunch, and Daniel insisted I put my feet up and rest awhile. Sharon came over while I rested and helped Daniel. She was an RN, so she could do all that Daniel required be done for his patients.

SEARCHING FOR MY MOUNTAIN

The ladies of the church fixed lunch for us and boxed us up some food for supper. They provided snacks for the people that came to see Daniel. I felt really good about the response we had.

We were just finishing cleaning up the trailer when we heard a knock on the back door where the patients had come in all day.

"Sharon or Lori must have forgotten something." I started to get up, but Daniel motioned for me to stay seated.

"I'll get it," he said, already half way to the door.

"What did you..." he stopped in mid sentence realizing it was neither Lori nor Sharon.

"Is there something we can do for you?" I heard him ask.

My curiosity got the better of me and I joined Daniel at the door.

A woman that looked not much older than Daniel and me stood at the door.

"My name is Iona Lewis. I live close by and I really need to speak to Dr. Scott. They said he would be here today."

"I'm Dr' Scott, but we are through seeing patients for the day."

"Ya see, I couldn't come till it was a gettin' dark, 'cause I didn't want nobody seein' me. I'm real skeert."

"Come in and have a seat," Daniel said gently.

The last thing Daniel and I needed was another patient, but hadn't we just prayed that morning that God would send people to us that needed us? Well, here she was.

She sat down in the chair opposite Daniel and me. She seemed to be visibly shaken and nervous. She kept wringing her hands together.

I went over and knelt down in front of her and took her hands in mine.

"It will be okay. Just tell us what we can do to help."

"I don't rightly know wher' to start. It's the baby; it's been cryin' fer three days a runnin'."

"How old is the baby?" Daniel asked.

"She's six months old, almost seven."

"Why didn't you bring her with you?"

"Oh, she ain't mine. She's my sister's baby. I don't know what it is, but there's sumpthin' bad. I just know."

"Is she running fever?"

"Hot as a poker at times, then it'll break, and she'll be cool fer a little bit. I've been after Essie to get her to somebody, but all she says is 'mind my own business', that she be taken care of it. She says it's just a teethin' and that's

140

all. But, Dr. Scott, I ain't never heared no baby cry that hard all the time from just cuttin' teeth.

"Essie's the baby's mother?"

"Yeah, she is."

"It sounds like she doesn't want you involved. There's nothing I can do to change that. I can't make her bring the baby to me."

"Don't ya see, it ain't her, it's that man of her'n. She's skeert to death of him. He beats her and the younguns all the time. He's mighty mean. 'Specially when he's been on the bottle, which is about all the time."

"How many children does she have?"

"She has the baby, Melissa, and a little boy, Ronnie, that's almost three, and another little boy, Andrew, five, and a little girl, Hannah, who's twelve."

"You know, Iona, that we just can't go up there and check their baby unless they ask us," Daniel lamented.

"I was thinkin' maybe ya could go and say yer givin' shots to the babies or sumpthin', and ask to give the baby a shot."

"What makes you think they would even let me see her?" he asked.

"We can't go tonight. I've got to get my wife home. She's having a baby and needs to get her rest. We'll go home and talk about a plan."

"Please, Dr. Scott, I don't think the little girl can stand much more," she said with tears in her eyes.

"Could you give us a few minutes to talk?" I asked Iona.

"Sure."

We went into the examining room and shut the door.

"What are we going to do, Daniel? This is a real crisis."

"I've got to get you someplace to rest."

"There was a hotel back on the road. We could stay over and go see this baby tomorrow?"

"I'll have to call Chris and see if I could get it worked out for him to take my calls tomorrow. This was just supposed to be a one day thing," he said, running his hand trough his dark curls. "I don't know when I've been this tired."

I went to the back of his chair and rubbed his shoulders. He took my hand and pressed it to his lips.

"What are we going to tell her?" I asked gently.

"There is a baby out there that could die, and I'm a doctor, we've got to try, Elizabeth."

"Let's go talk to her," I said, opening the door.

"We'll be back over here at the same place about ten o'clock in the morning. Can you meet us here to show us the way?"

I saw new fear appear in her eyes. "No!" she said empathically. "You don't know what you're askin'. If Bob knowed I was here I would be dead. I've got to not be with you, but I could give you directions to their house. It'll be easy to find."

"Are you close enough to see their house?"

"Yeah, I'm right on the same side of the road."

"Could you call the police if there is trouble?"

"Ani't nobody got no phones up there."

"Great!" Daniel exclaimed.

"Honey, we have the two way radio in here, couldn't you call the emergency channel with that."

"Yeah, that would work, but if we can't get to it, it won't do us any good," he interjected.

"Daniel, we're just going to have to trust God to take care of us."

"Honey, would you get Iona some paper and pencil, and let her write the directions down."

I got some paper off his work station and handed it to her. She took it tentatively.

143

"I can't write," she said, hanging her head with shame.

A tear escaped down her face. Her rough, calloused hand was quick to wipe it away.

"That's okay, sweetie, you tell me and I'll write it down," I said, trying to hide the emotion I felt for her.

"Do you know anything about these hills around here?" she asked.

"No, I'm afraid we don't."

"You go out here in front of the church and go up the road. You'll go about three mile, then you'll come to a store called County Line Store, ya turn right there. You won't go far 'til ya come to a bridge, go across it and turn up the next road. It'll wind up around this mountainside. You'll pass a big white farm house, and that un's mine, you can see Esther's house right next to mine. That's Essie's full name. I gotta go. I been gone way too long."

She got up and started to the door. I arose before her and put my arms around her. The tears she had tried so hard to fight back now were released into sobs. As I held her to me, the odor of her unkempt body hit my pregnant condition. Nausea attacked me with a vengeance. I pushed by her to try to make it to the little bathroom in the back of the trailer, and reached the commode just in time. After getting everything settled down again, I made my way back toward them and met Daniel coming down the hall.

"Are you okay, sweetie?"

I nodded my head as he pulled me into his arms. "I'm so embarrassed. I lost it when her body odor hit me. You know how smells get to me quicker than anything. I wanted to comfort her and look what I did. She must think I'm terrible. It was obvious what happened."

"No, she didn't think that. I reminded her about your pregnancy, and I prayed for her safety. She felt better when she left."

"I feel better now, too." I said, smiling at him.

"We just need to go to the hotel and eat supper. Then I'm calling Chris."

We got buckled into our seat and headed out to the hotel. It was nine o'clock by the time we got into our room. The cold plate they fixed for us was good. My nausea had abated and I was famished.

"I'm asking Chris to come," Daniel said.

"Here?" I asked in amazement.

"I'm asking him to go with us to these people's house. I don't want you involved, because you and the babies could get hurt."

"I don't think that will be necessary," I said curtly. "I'm not sick, Daniel; you're treating me like a child. I can do this job! You don't have to call Chris."

"I'm not saying you aren't capable, I'm just saying this could be a very dangerous situation. God gave you and these babies to me, and I have to protect you the best

145

way I know how. I am calling Chris!" he said, reaching for the phone as he spoke.

I knew from the sound of his voice he was going to be as stubborn as I. I flipped over with my back to him and pulled the cover up around my head. This was the closest we had ever come to actually being mad at each other. Unbidden tears slipped down my cheek. This pregnancy had made me so emotional. I quickly wiped them off with the corner of the sheet so he wouldn't know I had been crying.

"Chris, it's Daniel here."

"We're still here at Mount Laurel. We ran into kind of a problem..." I listened as he conveyed what had happened and asked him to come.

I heard him in the shower and tried to go to sleep before he came back in, but couldn't. I was too upset to calm down. I knew he was right. I needed to think about the babies. I was just so used to going long hours and being efficient. I felt like a failure.

He turned out the light and slipped under the cover beside me. I wanted him to hold me, but I wasn't going to make the first move. For the first time in our marriage, he turned his back to go to sleep. Evidently he wasn't going to disturb my pouting. I lay there in the darkness, suddenly very lonely in our king size bed. A new wave of tears started. I turned over on my back and reached out for Daniel. He turned toward me and without a word took me into his arms. He just held me until my tears were dried.

"Daniel?"

"Huh?"

"I just wanted you to be proud of me and see that I could handle whatever it was we would have to face, and all I managed to do was throw up on one of our new patients."

I heard him chuckle as he pulled me closer. "Honey you did a great job. I saw how professional you were with all the patients today, and I saw your gentleness. I haven't worked with anyone as good or as cute as you are."

"You're just saying that because you have to," I mumbled into his chest.

"I can't win. So you'll just have to believe me."

"Daniel?"

"Huh…" he returned sleepily.

"I was so proud of you today. It's the first time I've seen you be a doctor."

"Thank you, but you're only saying that to make me feel good."

"Okay, you got me," I said, laughing at him.

"Daniel, I don't like it when we're mad at each other."

"I wasn't mad, were you?"

"Yes you were. You've never gotten into bed and turned your back on me."

"I didn't think you wanted to be bothered. You had your back turned to me and your head covered up."

"But you knew I wanted you to hold me."

"I can't read your mind. Give me a break I'm really new at this. So if I'm right, when you get in bed and turn your back to me I'm supposed to know that you really want me to hold you. That makes a lot of sense to me."

"I'm sorry; I did get frustrated with you, but not mad. There's a difference."

"Okay, I was frustrated with you too, but not mad. I think we were upset over different things. I was upset because you were going to put you and the babies in jeopardy, and you were because you didn't think that I thought you could do the job. Am I right?"

"You're right."

"And I will tell you this right now, I will protect you and my babies until the day I die," he said, pulling me closer to him.

"I'll try hard to not resist. I've been on my own so long I forgot how it was to have a protector."

"When we said our vows at the altar, God transferred you into my hands, and I take that very seriously."

He placed his hand on my stomach above our babies. "That was why I hesitated about going up there. If I went into something that made you lose our children, I would die."

"I know, and I won't do anything stupid. I love you so much, I felt so lonely awhile ago over on the other side of the bed. Would you have gone to sleep and not have hugged me?"

"No, I knew you would turn over."

"Why were you so certain?"

"I knew that I just needed to give you some space, so I gave you some."

"I don't need space, I need you," I said, shifting my body closer to his.

"And I need you, Elizabeth," he said, smothering me with kisses.

We were lost in the sweet ocean of love that God made so beautiful. All the tiredness and frustrations of the day ebbed away as we were swept along in the current of its flow.

Later, as we lay in each other's arms, all seemed right with the world.

The sound of Daniel's breathing told me he was sleeping. I had gotten used to those comforting sounds. His hand rested on my stomach where he liked to lay it as he went to sleep.

"You're daddy loves you, little ones," I silently told my babies. "He will always be there to protect you and care for you." I wondered how my mother felt when she found out she was pregnant. How she must have loved me as she carried me. I had thought often of her since I found out I was pregnant. I had Daniel; she didn't have anyone. I would rather have him overprotective than not have anyone. I drifted off to sleep, content in the arms of my love.

Daniel had already showered and was ready to go before he woke me. I opened my eyes to feel his kisses on my face.

"Good morning, my princess," he said, pushing my hair back from my face.

"What time is it? Am I late?"

"No, you're fine. I got up early to read the Bible and pray. I figured we might need and extra measure of grace today."

"I'm so tired this morning."

"I know, that's why I let you sleep. We had a busy day and night."

"I'm barely into my fourth month with this pregnancy and I'm already tired. I hope this isn't a bad sign."

"In the first three or four months you are more tired because your body is adjusting to such an awesome

150

task. There is a miracle taking place in your womb. As you sleep, God is doing some awesome things with our babies. I was just reading in the scripture about how God works in the secret parts of the womb to do marvelous and wonderful works. He knew our children before we conceived them," he said, his eyes filled with the emotion of it all.

"I love you so much, Dr. Scott."

He didn't say another word, just climbed in bed beside me and held me for a long while.

"I need to get up soon and hop in the shower. Maybe it will wake me up."

"We might need to rethink your doing all this until the babies are born," he said gently.

I knew he might be right. I got silently out of bed and headed to the shower. The thought of my dream going to someone else seemed so unfair, and I didn't want someone else sharing all of this with Daniel. I pushed it to the back of my mind and let the hot, steamy water flow over me. I suddenly felt something that seemed like a flutter in my stomach. I turned off the shower so everything would be totally quiet. I waited and felt nothing again, I was about to give up and call it gas when it happened once more. I screamed for Daniel to come into the bathroom.

"What? What's the matter?" he said, visibly shaken as he reached me. "Answer me, what's wrong?" He took me by my shoulders and looked deep into my eyes.

"I just felt one of the babies move," I said with tears running down my face. "I just felt life inside me."

He grabbed a towel and put it around my shoulders. "You scared me to death. I thought you had a problem. I feel week as a kitten," he said, leaning up against the bathroom wall.

"Daniel, did you hear what I said?" I asked. "I felt one of our babies move".

"I heard what you said. I'm just trying to switch from being scared to death to being overjoyed. You're going to kill me before the babies get here," he said, holding his hand over his heart.

"This is the first time I've ever felt this. It's like a little kiss from heaven," I said, with water dripping down out of my hair.

"What does it feel like?"

"It feels like a butterfly fluttering around," I said, smiling.

"Do you think I could feel it?" Daniel asked excitedly.

"No, it's too deep, but you can listen to the heartbeat later," I said, kissing him.

"You get all the fun," he said. "Run along and get dressed. I need to go pull the trailer around."

I hurried and dried my hair and dressed. I was ready to go in no time. I told Daniel I would put some make up on in the trailer while he found a place for breakfast. We found the Hardee's where we got our food the morning before.

"What's our plan, Daniel?" I asked between bites of my sausage and egg biscuit.

"Chris will be at the church at 9:00. I guess we'll make final plans when he gets here. How do you feel today?"

"I feel great, no nausea this morning. I just hope I don't barf today. Do you think it's early for me to feel the babies move?"

"Not with twins. They take up more space, so you would feel them sooner."

"Today has been a good day," I said, smiling at him.

"I hope that's the way it ends," he said on a serious note.

We pulled into the church parking lot to wait for Chris. It was ten till nine, so if he was on time he should be here any minute.

"I'm going to work on some of the paper work from yesterday," I said, heading to the back.

"We didn't get much done last night, did we?" he said with smile.

"Actually, we did. We had our first fight, and made up. That took up most of the night.

"It wasn't a fight, it was a discussion." he added.

"Okay, whatever it was, it was fun making up afterward," I said, smiling.

"Okay, here's file one, Jake and Ida Sowers," I added, handing the folder to him.

"I didn't have time to talk to you about these two. I have a feeling Jake is in for some heavy duty problems. His prostate is way too large. I'm hoping antibiotics are going to work for him, but I think it could be cancer. I didn't want to hop into radical treatment too quickly, but in two weeks if I don't see change I'm going to have to send him to the hospital. I guess if I send him, Ida will have to go with him. Those two make such a cute couple."

"What did he whisper to you about doing it?"

"That's patient privacy. You know that."

"Do they?"

"Actually they do. Isn't that good to know? I hope when we get that old we still do it."

"Oh, Daniel, you embarrass me sometimes."

Chris came in just as I was finishing my statement.

"I can embarrass you all the time. Want me to try?" he said, leaning over and kissing my cheek.

"How's the little mama?"

"The little mama felt one of the babies move this morning," Daniel said, smiling up at Chris.

"No way, isn't this early to be feeling movement? I'm not up to snuff on my obstetrics, but isn't it?"

"That's right; I haven't talked to you lately to tell you our other news. I counted two heartbeats the other night."

"No way!" he exclaimed grinning from ear to ear.

"Way, he was trying to find a third one and was so disappointed he only found two. I told him he acted like he was hunting Easter eggs," I said, laughing.

"Do twins run in your family?"

"Well believe it or not, I'm a twin of a sister." I held my hand up before he could say it. "I know, no way."

"You took the words right out of my mouth. Where is she, are you keeping her from me?"

"You can date her when you get to heaven. She died during childbirth."

"Oh, I'm sorry, I didn't know."

"Neither did I until right before Christmas."

"No way," we all said in unison.

"You are loaded with info today, girl."

"My mother died in childbirth and my I was raised by another woman."

"So, don't twins skip a generation?"

"Evidently not." I said, smiling at him.

"You know what, putting all kidding aside; we seriously have to talk about your health. You know that I think a section is the only way to go."

"Daniel thinks so, too."

"And what does Elizabeth think?" Chris asked, looking directly at me.

"Elizabeth thinks she has some mighty good doctors and she ought to take their advice," I said, smiling at Daniel.

"How do you feel?" Chris questioned.

"You and Daniel are going to drive me nuts before they get here."

"You ain't seen nothin' yet, baby."

"I was really tired last night. How many patients did we see yesterday, Daniel?"

"Elizabeth said fifty some, but I only counted forty folders."

"Man! That was a good turnout for the first visit. What kind of patients?"

"Old, young, pregnant, you name it; we saw 'em. I was pleased with the number of pregnancies that came through. At least they're seeking early prenatal care," Daniel said.

"What's going on with this case today? Talk to me, do you have a gun?"

"I'm a doctor, not a sheriff. To answer your question, no, I don't have one with me."

"I think maybe you better start carrying one. Just make sure it's out of sight and away from any kids."

"I know how to care for one, I just never thought of needing one. Now, I think I'm about to change my mind."

"What happened last night?"

"There was a knock about seven or so and the lady looked upset. So we invited her in and she said her niece had been crying incessantly. I think she said about three or four days. She has been running fever off and on. The problem is the parents don't think she needs to see a doctor. Iona (the aunt) says the father is very abusive when he drinks. He evidently beats the crap out of his wife and kids, and threatens to kill the relatives. There are four children ranging from six or eight months to twelve. There's two little boys."

"So maybe this won't be as bad as Iona thinks it will be."

"Iona suggested we go to the house and tell them we're out and about giving kids their shots."

"That sounds good. It just might work."

"Do you have the directions?"

"Yeah, here they are." I said, handing them to him.

"Well, let's go do it."

"Let's pray first," Daniel suggested.

"Good idea."

"Father, protect us as we go. Go before us and prepare the way. Help us be a blessing today. Amen."

"Chris you can set up front with Daniel and read him directions. I'll sit back here and do records."

It didn't take long for us to reach the place where we turned at the store to go up the mountainside. Iona's directions were distinct, and we didn't have any problems.

I cleared away the folders and stored them for transfer. Everything looked neat and tidy. I hoped the visit was smooth for everyone.

I looked out the window and saw the white farm house that Iona lived in. I thought I saw a curtain move in what appeared to be the kitchen window. The house we pulled up to was a rundown, dilapidated old shack. The boards that were once white hung with peeling and blistered paint, and some windows were missing. An old sofa and lounge chair sat on the front porch. Chickens were pecking around in the barren yard. Where a picket fence used to be, slats were lying here and there, all the way around the yard. The front gate was still closed, with no fencing on either side. It seemed the only thing that was fully intact was the front gate.

I heard the barking of several dogs. I didn't see any, so I supposed they were tied.

"Libby, now that I have thought about it, maybe it would be good for you to go in with me. It would be less alarming for them. And you're so cute, who would want to hurt you."

"So you're going to make me walk in front?" I exclaimed.

"You don't think I would want to be first, do you?" he said, winking at Chris.

Daniel got his doctor bag and we proceeded to the front door. I could still hear the dogs bark, but didn't see any. Mountain dogs scared me the most because they were trained to hunt and protect rather than be cuddly companions. I saw the ragged curtain pull back and two dirty little faces peer out.

Daniel knocked on the door. We waited and no one came. He rapped again and we waited some more. Finally the door cracked open just about two inches.

"We don't want nuthin'," I heard her say.

"Ma'am, my name is Dr. Scott, and this is my wife, Elizabeth. We're not selling anything, we're just checking to see if any of the children are in need of their baby shots. I see you have children," he said.

We could hear her baby crying all the way out on the porch.

"My babies don't need nuthin'."

As she shifted the baby in her arms, the door came open a little farther.

"You sure do have a pretty little baby there. She seems to not be feeling well. Do you think she might need for me to check her? It won't cost you anything."

I saw her demeanor soften some as I talked to her. The baby continued to scream as she patted her back.

"I wouldn't mind stepping in for just a minute since we're here anyway."

I could see her waffling as she stood there. I prayed she wouldn't turn us away. Just looking at the baby, I could tell she was in distress. Her face was flushed and looked feverish. Esther appeared frightened, but reluctantly invited us in.

"Has your baby been sick very long?" Daniel quizzed her.

"It's just her teeth fixin' to come in. They'll be in soon and she'll be better.

We were working our way up to checking the baby when we heard a piercing scream come from the back room. Our heads jerked around toward the direction of the eerie sound. I caught Daniel's eye and saw the alarm that crossed his face.

"Don't pay no 'teniton, it's just them kids fightin' agin. They do that all the time."

About the time she finished her sentence, a young girl came stumbling into the room holding her stomach and screaming in agony.

"Mama he'p me I'm hurtin' bad," she said, holding tight to her stomach as she fell. She lay writhing on the wooden floor.

Daniel rushed to her side. He told her that he was a doctor and could help her. "Turn over and let me see what this pain could be," he said gently.

Her pain seemed to lessen after a minute or so. I could tell that she was no more than eleven or twelve, at the most, a skinny little girl with a protruding stomach. I knew this had to be Hannah. He was trying to feel of her belly when she grabbed Daniel as if he could free her of this demon that had gripped her body. Terror filled her little eyes as the pain gripped her again.

"He'p me, please, please he'p me," she screamed again.

"We're going to help you, baby. Just hold on until I can see what's happening, okay?" Daniel smoothed the hair from her sweaty face, talking calmly as he tried to do a visual exam.

"I'm going to take you to our trailer outside so I can check you better. Okay?"

As he lifted her off the floor there was a circle of blood where she had lain.

"Elizabeth, go tell Chris I'm coming, and to get ready for me. We have a problem."

I rose to go and heard a booming voice behind me.

"Move her ya die."

We heard the cocking of a gun and as we turned toward the sound we looked up into the end of a double-barrel shotgun.

"Sir, is this your little girl?" Daniel asked calmly.

"What's it to ya?" he slurred.

I could tell he was very drunk.

Suddenly the scream came again, piercing the air around us.

"Daddy, daddy, please let him he'p me, I'm hurtin'. I'm gonna die, I know it, I'm gonna die," she yelled at him.

Daniel lifted the little girl in his arms and stood to face the drunken man.

"Elizabeth I want you to slowly move in behind me. We are going to walk to the door," he said, as much to the man as to me.

My heart was racing as the adrenalin pumped through my body.

Daniel kept staring at the man as he backed out of the house. Their eyes were locked on each other. The little

162

girl had fainted in his arms. Her once ridged body was now limp in his arms.

"I have a trailer right outside. I can take care of her there. I'm not going to hurt her. She's real sick; I've got to help her."

The man didn't say whether we could go or not. We just backed out of the house. Once we were outside, Daniel and I ran into the trailer with the little girl.

"What the hell?" Chris exclaimed as we rushed in with the little girl.

"I don't know what we have here, but she's bleeding and screaming with pain," Daniel said, headed to the rear operating suite.

I grabbed the scissors and began cutting her clothing off. All of my trauma training just seemed to kick in. I hooked up the blood pressure cuff and got an IV started. The room was small, so I stepped back to give Chris and Daniel room to work.

She came out of her fainting spell as the pain gripped her again and the screaming started over. With terror still in her eyes, she looked helplessly at Daniel, begging him to stop the pain.

A gush of water came from under her.

The horror of what was wrong with her hit us all at the same time.

"Damn!" Chris said. "She's having a baby.

I had exam gloves ready for Daniel and Chris to slip into. I helped them get her legs into the stirrups at the end of the table.

Daniel examined her internally as he pressed gently on her stomach.

"She's about seven centimeters. Elizabeth, go get me the stethoscope that I listened to the babies with. It's in the front of the trailer. I need to see if I can get a heartbeat."

"Doctor? The little girl moaned. "What's wrong? Can you make the pain leave?"

"What's your name, sweetie?"

"Hannah," she said through the snubbing of her crying.

"Hannah, honey, do you know what having a baby means?"

About that time another contraction started.

"It's coming again! It's coming again!" she screamed, grabbing Daniel's hand.

Chris slipped some of the pain medication into her IV.

"This should help in just a second, sweetheart," Chris crooned to her.

"The contraction is going away now. Your pain is going back down now."

"Hannah, do know what's happing to you? Daniel asked as he listened for a heartbeat.

She shook her head. She still had the wild look of an animal getting caught in a trap.

"You're going to have a baby. We can't make the pain go away, but we *are* going to help you through it."

New sobs gripped her body.

"You can put some valium in with pain meds," Daniel told Chris.

"I've already done that."

"I should have known that," Daniel said, forcing a smile.

"Are you a doctor, too?" Hannah said, looking at Chris.

"Yeah, I come along to make sure Dr. Daniel treats you right," he said, winking her.

"Will you help me keep him straight?" Chris asked her.

"I want my mama," she said, holding her hand tight over her eyes.

"We'll get her in a little bit, okay?"

"I get a faint heartbeat way down low. I think we're going to be in for a breach," Daniel said, shaking his head. "We need her mama. We may have to do a C-section

165

Chris, and we can't without permission from someone."
He removed his gloves and threw them into the trash can.
I thought I had seen him angry before, but never had I
seen him like this.

"Daniel, he has a gun, you know. You can't risk
going in there again," I shouted at him out of sheer panic.

"That little girl is going to die if I don't," he said as
he started out the door.

"And my baby's father might if he goes in there," I
said, my voice getting quieter.

He hesitated for a second and slammed the door as
he went to get Esther.

"Oh, God send your angels to protect him," I
prayed.

I saw out the window that Esther had met Daniel in
the yard and was coming to the trailer with him.

"Bob is gone; he's not in the house anymore. We're
safe right now," Daniel said, coming into the trailer.

He came to me and gave me a reassuring hug. "I'm
sorry, but I had no choice. I desperately need your
prayers."

We heard a scream coming from the back room
again.

"Esther, Hannah is having a baby, and you need to
go say something to her. She wants you."

Daniel headed full speed back to where Hannah lay on the table. He and Chris both were trying to help her through the contraction.

"What'll I say?" Esther sobbed.

"Did you know she was pregnant?" I questioned.

She nodded her head.

"Didn't you tell her anything?" I asked.

"I didn't know what to do."

"Stop crying!" I demanded, shaking her shoulders. "You've got a baby back there that doesn't have a clue what's happening to her. You dry those tears and go back there and help her."

The latest contraction was beginning, and tension was high as we entered the room.

"Mama!" she cried out when she saw her.

"Did what daddy did make a baby?" she questioned her mother.

"I'm so sorry, honey. I was afraid of 'im too," she said, leaning down to hug her. They sobbed in each other's arms.

"He won't hurt ya no more. I promise. He ain't comin' back, sweetie. You rest now, I gotta go get Melissa Ann, she's a sleepin', and the boys."

"Don't go, Mama, I'm skeert."

167

"I'm takin' the kids to Iona's, and I'll be right back," she said, kissing her forehead.

Daniel followed her into the hallway.

"Dr. Thomas and I may have to do surgery to deliver the baby. We talked it over and we're sure we have everything to do it. Do we have your permission? If we don't, she may die."

She nodded her head and left the trailer.

Daniel had just finished with another internal exam when I entered.

"She's a ten, and can push if we let her. We've got to make a decision Chris. I say let her try pushing some and see if she can do it. We would be in much better shape if we didn't have to do a section."

"You're the doctor," Chris said, yielding the choice to Daniel.

"Hannah, when your next pain comes, I want you to push down like you do when you go poop."

"I like your medical terms," Chris said, smiling at him.

"I figured she wouldn't have a clue what a bowel movement was," Daniel returned.

"Elizabeth, would you get Chris and me set up for surgery. We will need it as sterile as possible. You remember the procedure we went through the other day?"

"Yes, it's already done."

"I told you she was good," Chris said to Daniel. "I've seen her in action, you haven't."

"I beg to differ," Daniel said.

The contraction was starting. Daniel positioned himself at the end of the table to watch the progress. She pushed for over an hour with no success.

"I cain't do it no more, Dr. Daniel. I cain't do it no more," she wailed. "Just pull it out, please, just pull it out."

"Daniel, her blood pressure is unstable," Chris said.

"Sweetheart, just close your little eyes. We're going to let you rest. When you wake up from your sleep, it will all be over," Daniel said, patting her arm.

"Promise?" she said, grabbing his hand and staring into his eyes to see if he was telling the truth.

Chris was already administering the anesthesia.

"Are you getting sleepy?" Daniel asked.

She looked up at him and smiled the sweetest little smile.

"Thank you," she said as her eyes fluttered. "No more pain," she mumbled weakly.

"That's right, honey, no more pain," Daniel answered, struggling to keep the emotion from his voice. He stroked her hair as she went into a deeper sleep.

I already had her stomach scrubbed and ready for the procedure by the time she was totally under.

I put my gown and mask on and helped the guys with theirs.

"Would you like to cut?" Daniel asked Chris, since he was a surgeon.

"If you want me to, but I think you're more than capable."

"Elizabeth, you watch her meds and vitals and Chris will help me. When we deliver the baby you're going to have to help with it. Okay?"

"Right." I nodded as he pulled the bright light down and position it above her stomach.

I had already gotten the other exam room ready for the little one.

All was quiet except for the banter between the doctors as they worked to get to the baby.

"She is so small; there isn't much space to work in here," Daniel said, trying to wiggle the baby out.

"How's she doing, honey?" Daniel asked.

"Her blood pressure has come down some since she's asleep. But everything looks stable," I answered.

170

They birthed the butt first. "It's a little boy," Daniel said, lifting him the rest of the way out.

There was a gasp from Daniel as he turned the baby over. His little face was grotesquely deformed. By the time he had cut the cord, there was no heartbeat. There was no life in the little baby. His tiny limbs flopped as Daniel moved him.

"Elizabeth, you need to leave the room. Chris and I can finish. You don't need to see this," he demanded.

He didn't have to tell me twice. Nausea hit me full force and I headed to the bathroom down the hall.

After throwing up all I had on my stomach, I just sat down on the commode and sobbed. I held my hand over my stomach where my own babies lay, and begged God to make them healthy.

After he was finished, Daniel carried Hannah into one of the other exam rooms that had a more comfortable bed. Chris was right behind with the IV bag. She was waking up some from the anesthesia, and was beginning to moan.

I looked in the intake room of the trailer and saw that Esther was back and sitting quietly with her hands folded in her lap. I went to her and told her that Hannah was okay, but they had to do a C-section. Her eyes were red and swollen from crying. "Can I see her?" she asked quietly.

"I'll go ask Daniel," I said, and patted her hand as I went into the other room.

I closed the door behind me. Daniel was sitting beside her, taking her vitals as I came in.

"How is she? Her mom wants to know."

"She's trying to wake up, but we're going to keep her pretty sedated until we can get her to a hospital. Chris went up front to call a rescue squad and the police," he said quietly. I could see that he was totally drained. "Her blood pressure is still on the high side, but considering all she's been through it isn't surprising."

"Are you okay?" I asked, putting my hand on his shoulder.

He reached up and put his hand on mine. "They don't teach this stuff in med school. I'm sorry you had to see the baby. I tried to send you out before you got a good look at him."

"I'm fine, down a meal or two, but other than that, I'm fine."

"Libby, you did such a superb job today," he said, smiling at me.

We heard a light tap on the door and Chris entered.

"How's the patient?" he inquired.

"I was telling Elizabeth that her pressure is still up, but it's nothing I didn't expect. I'm going to keep her pretty much out until we can get her outta here," Daniel told him.

"I thought you might want to know that the other lady that is the sister to Hannah's mom, she's out in the waiting room with a crying baby."

"I forgot about the other kids..." he exclaimed and jumped up. "Bring her back to the other exam room. I wonder where her boys are."

"Libby, could you watch Hannah for me while I go check the baby?"

"Sure."

I went and got Hannah's mother to come in and sit by her.

"She will rest comfortably until the rescue squad comes," I told her. "Your sister said you had two boys. Where are they?"

"Iona took them over to her house. Her teenage daughter's there with 'em. Wher's Hannah's baby?" Esther asked.

"The baby died," I said gently.

"Oh," was all she said aloud. "It's prob'ly just as well," she muttered to herself.

I went in to check on Daniel and Chris. The little girl had cried so much that her cry was raspy. They had all her clothing off except her diaper.

"What did you find?" I asked.

"Nothing so far," they said in unison.

173

"Your two big guys look cute with that little baby," I said smiling at them.

"Okay, let's take the diaper off and I'll check her stomach area. It could be appendicitis."

Daniel removed her diaper and saw dried blood.

"Oh God, don't let this be what I think it is." Daniel moaned.

He spread her little legs and she cried out in pain. He separated her as much as he could.

"She's swollen badly. There's blood caked around her genitals, see Chris," Daniel said.

"It looks like she could be infected. No wonder she's crying. An animal wouldn't do this," Chris returned.

"Honey, there's some numbing solution in that drawer, could you hand it to me?"

"Sure." I looked over his shoulder as he doctored the little girl.

"What was her temp, Chris?"

"103 point two."

"Chris, could you get her some pain meds ready for an injection and a syringe of penicillin? She's going to love us," Daniel said to no one in particular. "That will keep her comfortable until we can get her to a hospital. She's probably ripped inside."

"You know she is?" he said, shaking his head.

Our heads jerked up and we all jumped at the sound of the shotgun going off.

"Was that a gun?" Chris asked.

"I hope he's not coming in here. Go lock the door, Chris," Daniel demanded. "The police should be here soon."

"Esther, would your husband come in here shooting?" I asked her from the hall.

"He won't be botherin' nobody. He just kilt hisself. He told me was a gonna do it. I told him go ahead, then me and the kids would finally be free. I told him he better do a good job, 'cause I would finish it if he didn't. He knowed what was happenin' to the kids and he knowed he did it," she said with all emotion gone from her face.

Daniel took the sleeping baby and gave her Iona to hold.

"She's very sick. I gave her some medicine to help her rest until we get her to a hospital. Her fever was spiked and I gave her something to bring it down. I also gave her a big shot of antibiotic for her infection. She didn't like Dr. Scott too much by the time I finished with her." Daniel said smiling.

"I knowed sumpthin' bad was wrong with her. What was it, Dr. Scott?"

"She was raped," Daniel said with his voice breaking.

Iona drew the little sleeping girl close to her and sobbed into her blanket.

"I wasn't soon enough. I wasn't soon enough!" She repeated as she sobbed.

"If you hadn't had the courage to come to me when you did there would have been three dead children today. As it is we have only one, Hannah's."

"She had a youngun? Little Hannah had a youngun?" she said, confused at Daniel comment.

"You didn't know?"

She shook her head in disbelief. "They quit lettin' me come around. When I'd try, Essie wouldn't let me in."

"Did Essie know Hannah was gonna have a baby?" Iona questioned.

"Yeah, I guess she was scared to death to tell anyone, even Hannah..." he hesitated for a moment. "Even Hannah didn't know what was happening to her. She was terrified."

"We kinda suspected he was messin' with 'em, but you just don't jump in wher' ya ain't invited. You get mad, but just keep yer mouth shet. We all been messed with by somebody, Dr. Scott. Me and Esther both lived through things that would make you sick to yer stomick. We didn't have nobody to turn to. Nobody woulda believed us anyhow. We was just lucky we didn't have no younguns. People are jest like animals up here on this mountainside. They don't care who they hop on and ride: animals, kids, boys, girls, it never mattered. When they'd be drunk you knowed ya better hide till they get over it, but sometime there weren't no place to hide. Then you jest have to make yer mind take ya someplace wher' ya cain't be hurt."

"I'm sorry, Iona, I'm so sorry," Daniel said.

"Did you hear the shotgun, Dr. Scott? I came a runnin' when I heared it."

"Chris has gone to check, but Esther thinks he might have committed suicide."

"He did," Chris said, coming into the trailer. "Esther was dead on, pardon the pun," Chris said.

"You look like you saw a ghost," Daniel told Chris.

"It wasn't a pretty sight. I had to get close enough to see if he was living. There wasn't much left of his head." Chris grimaced at the thought.

"I was so skeert. I thought fer sure he kilt somebody. I woulda prayed if I was a prayin' person," Iona said.

Esther was sitting by Hannah in silence, just staring at her. We heard the ambulance coming up the road to the house. Hannah and the baby were still sleeping. Both finding respite from the awful pain they had suffered. Chris had prepared the dead baby for transport.

The police came in and took a report from all of us. Daniel explained that the children had been raped, supposedly by the father. The policeman let out an oath that would make a sailor blush. "He won't rape anymore," Chris said. "He blew his face off with a shotgun. He's back behind the house. I guess things caught up with him and he couldn't face it."

The policeman told his partner to go check it out.

"What a mess," the officer said, shaking his head as he continued to write.

"I need to ask Mrs. Luke some questions. Where is she?" he said curtly.

"Right this way. She's sitting with her daughter," Daniel said.

He showed him the way to the exam room where they were.

"Mrs. Luke, do you know what happed to your girls?" the policeman said, towering above her as she sat with her hands folded in her lap.

She barely nodded her head, never looking his way.

"So you knew that he had sex with both them?"

"He said he would kill me if I told. Then they woulda had nobody to hold 'em when he hurt 'em. I'm all they had." She said emotionless.

"I'm sorry to have to do this but you're going to have to come down to the office with me and answer some more questions."

She rose in robot fashion and walked to the waiting room. She didn't focus on anyone or anything.

Iona got to her feet and put her arms around her. "I'm so sorry Esther. I wish I had been sooner," she said, trying to control the sobs that had started in her throat. "I'll take care of the kid fer ya, and I'll be over to see ya." She sobbed as she held her sister.

She stood stiff and motionless in Iona arms, never acknowledging her presence.

Daniel mentioned to the police officer that he was concerned about her mental state. She seemed to have retreated to a place in her mind where the pain couldn't reach her anymore. She had become totally unresponsive by this time. There were no signs of life as Daniel shown a light into her eyes. She had shut down the line to wherever she had gone.

"Sometimes when the trauma is more than we can handle, it will just shut a person down. We have a lot to learn about the mind and how it works. She may never heal from this one. Maybe it's because she doesn't have to protect the kids anymore. She can finally take care of Esther. I just hope it isn't too late."

"You know we're going to have to take her in. She allowed this to happen to these little girls, so we've got to charge her with child neglect."

"You won't be able to communicate with her. The real criminal is dead, you know? She was a victim as much as the children were," Daniel said, taking her pulse.

"She's in a catatonic state right now. You aren't going to get any statement from her."

"We'll see that she gets taken care of. We'll probably carry her on down to the mental hospital."

Chris helped load Hannah and the baby Melissa. He filled the paramedics in on all we had done and gave them instructions for the ride to the hospital. Hannah hadn't roused enough to ask about the baby. She mumbled a couple of times for her mama.

The coroner took Bob Luke and the dead baby to the morgue. Iona still was trying to regain her composure.

"Dr. Scott, are you a prayin' man?" he asked.

"Yeah, we prayed a lot today, all three of us."

"Wher' was he at?" she asked, concentrating on the wringing of her hands.

"Where was who at?" Daniel responded.

"That God ya pray to, wher' was he at when this happened to the girls? Wher' was he at when me and Esther was raped all our lives. Does he even care about us hill people?"

"He was here, and still is here. If I could tell you why God allowed it to happen, I would, but I won't even pretend to know the answer. I do know what caused it to happen."

"I know what caused it," she returned. "It was that bastard, Bob Luke and his drinkin'."

"But what made him that way?"

180

"The bottle," she answered.

"It's sin, Iona, we are all born sinners. Satan controls people and they end up doing just what Bob Luke did."

"How come I ain't ever felt 'im, Dr. Scott? Am I so bad that he won't come to me?"

"No, it's because we are all bad that he came. Allow me to tell you a story, Iona. A long time ago, in the Garden of Eden, Adam and Eve sinned, and after that, ever child that has ever been born has been born a sinner. The wages or payment of this sin is death. That death is not dying like we die physically, but it's a spiritual death, an eternal separation from God. Then God sent his only son from heaven to come to earth to die on an old rugged cross. By doing this, we would have a payment for our sin that we were born into. Do you understanding what I'm saying?"

She nodded to let him know she did.

"There could only be one sacrifice for us, it had to be someone perfect without blemish. The only one that could do that was God's son, Jesus. He took all our sin on him the day he died on Calvary, and made a way for us to go to heaven. That's a gift from God to us. If I were to give you a gift, what would you have to do for it to be yours?"

"I guess I would have to take it from ya."

"That's the way salvation is. It's a gift to you from God. But for you to have it, you must accept it. If you never take it to yourself, it will never become yours. If I were to buy you a gift and you never took it from me, it would never be yours, even though it had your name on it. So even though Christ died for our sins, unless we take it, or ask for it, it will never be ours."

"So what yer sayin' is, if I want to have this gift of salvation all I have to do is ask fer it?" she said, nodding her head.

"That's what I'm saying. God makes it so simple that a child can understand."

"Why ain't nobody ever told me this before?" she said with a tear running down her cheek.

"I don't know the answer to that, but I do know that God sent me today to tell you about how much he loves you. All you have to do is pray and ask him. In Romans it says if you will confess with your mouth the Lord Jesus and believe in your heart that God has raised him from the dead, you shall be saved."

"What's Romans?"

I had gotten Daniel's Bible from the front of the trailer and handed it to him with the page open to the book of Romans.

"It's a book in the Bible. Look, it's right here," he said, turning it so she could see it.

"I ain't never had one of them. So does that mean I have to confess my sins? I have so many I cain't 'member 'em all," she said with an embarrassed little chuckle.

"No, what it means is that you confess that Jesus is your Lord, you tell people with your mouth that Jesus is your Savior. And if you believe that he died and rose again, and is in heaven with his Father, his word says he will save you. And that salvation is forever. He won't ever take it from you, because all your sin is covered by the blood of Christ."

"You mean that's all I have to do to know the Jesus you know? Will God hear my prayers then?"

Her eyes lit up with the news Daniel was telling her.

"Yes, he promised us he would, and he has never broken a promise."

"Would ya help me, Dr. Scott, to know your Savior?"

"We can pray right now. Would you like to?" Daniel asked expectantly.

"Yes," she said with tears running down her cheeks.

Daniel went through the sinner's prayer with her while Chris and I watched. I stood and listened in amazement as my husband led her to the Lord. A miracle took place as the two of them, on bended knee, asked for her salvation. I stole a look at Chris, and saw the tenderness in his eyes as he looked on the scene before us. We had melted into the background as the Holy Spirit worked in our midst. On that day, this gentle husband of mine had physically saved lives and had led a soul to the saving knowledge of Christ. This truly was a ministry that God could use to further the kingdom.

Chris and I knelt beside them in the small waiting room and rejoiced together in prayer for her new spiritual life.

"I feel so light inside. It's like I got butterflies goin' around my insides," she said as we got to our feet.

"You're now our sister in Christ," Daniel said as he hugged her.

"The sister of a doctor, who could imagine?" she said, smiling.

"But better still, you are a sister to Christ and all that is his is yours to share with him when we all get to heaven."

"Maybe this will be a start of healin' here on this sin-cursed mountain," she said, wiping the tears from her eyes.

"The girls are going to need a lot of love as they get better. And Esther's boys have also been affected. Their father is dead and it's hard to say when their mom will come home. All they've known has been ripped from them. You will be able to tell them that Jesus loves them. They are so young to have suffered so much. Melissa Ann probably won't remember much, but Hannah is going to need a lot of help from you. Find you a good church so you can grow in the Lord."

"I guess I better git on down to the house. The kids will prob'ly be needin' me. My daughter, Susan, is a watchin' 'em. I'll never be able to pay ya fer all ya done fer me, but I guess now I can be prayin' fer ya. Mrs. Scott, ya take keer of yerself and them younguns ya got growin' inside ya."

"I will, Iona. Maybe after they're born, Daniel and I will bring them to see you."

"You would do that fer me?"

"We sure would," Daniel added. "After all, we have to keep tabs on the girls to see how they are mending."

"Bye now," she said, going down the steps.

"Iona, wait. I have something for you." Daniel turned and got his Bible off the table and handed it to her.

"Oh, Dr. Scott, I cain't take it, it yers."

"I have another one. I think you might want to read some of the stories in here. It will help you get to know about Jesus."

With tears in her eyes, she accepted the gift Daniel offered her. She hugged it to her and walked silently down the dusty road toward home. Freer than she'd ever been in her life.

The three of us just sat and looked from one to the other.

"It's been one helluv a day," Chris piped up, breaking the silence.

"That's exactly what it's been, directly from hell. That's how all of this happened. Because of Satan and the hell he came from. It gets into people and they do things like what has happened here today," Daniel said. "And we saw hell defeated when Iona accepted the Lord as Savior."

"I've never witnessed a soul being saved before, except mine, that is," Chris said.

"I never expected to be doing that. It just started in an innocent conversation and the Holy Spirit took over. I haven't led a soul to Christ in a long time. It's a humbling experience."

"I've never led a soul to Christ. I'm ashamed to say. I guess I've never known how. Of course I haven't been close enough to him over the years to be of any service. If I had, my marriage would not have ended. I put my work ahead of everything and I lost a lot."

"But it isn't too late," I added.

"The experience I had with you and almost losing you was what turned my life around. I witnessed a miracle, and I recognized it as such. There was nothing I could do to save you, and I knew it. When I operated on you, it was really for Daniel, because I knew he loved you so much. I knew in my heart of hearts you were as much as gone. Not that I didn't give it one hundred percent. It was when I knew there was no hope and God healed you that I was changed forever. I saw Daniel never give up. He prayed all the time and let me know that. When things were so bleak, he was still begging God for you. And I kept seeing you hang on, and he kept praying and you kept hanging, and then it happened, you opened your eyes. That was the moment I knew I had to be with you

186

guys, and have what you have. I had to make something count for someone other than myself."

"And here you are witnessing some more miracles."

"I'm glad you called me last night. It's been a horribly wonderful day."

"I couldn't have expressed it any better," Daniel added.

"Guys, we need to go home," I interjected.

"You're right. Let's get this baby home," Daniel said.

"Don't say baby," Chris said.

"I've got three babies to get home, two little ones and the one carrying them," Daniel said, smiling at me.

"I'll help you get the trailer cleaned up and back in shape tomorrow after I sleep in. I've had them transport Hannah and the baby to our hospital," Chris said.

"So that means one of us is going to have to go by the hospital before we go home," Daniel surmised.

"No, what I did was, I told them to call Roger. He's the one that could handle this better than we can. The baby is probably going to have to have surgery," Chris said.

"Great, now we can go home," I sighed.

Daniel came and hugged me.

"Yeah, I think that's a good idea."

We took Chris back to the church to get his car and we headed home. It seemed like we had been gone for several days. I couldn't wait to get home to my bed.

Chapter Seven

We arrived back at our house at 10:00 o'clock. We dragged ourselves out of the trailer and up the stairs to our room. After a quick shower we snuggled down under the cover. I felt a baby move, and took Daniel's hand and placed it over the area where I felt it.

"I know you can't feel it but I want you to know where the little flutter is," I said, moving his hand to the area.

"I wish I could feel what you're feeling," he said wistfully.

"When I saw that little baby today, I thought for a moment..."

"Shhh...Don't even think that, sweetheart. Our babies are going to be beautiful just like their mother. We can't worry over things that are beyond our control. Hannah's baby was probably deformed from incest. I've read some studies on that."

"Our first trip will be a memorable one."

"I hope and pray this isn't an omen," he said with a chuckle.

"I was so proud of you today. You made me feel so safe. Your decisions were made without hesitation. You were so sure of yourself."

"If you only knew what went through my brain today. The last thing I wanted to do was to operate on that little girl, but I knew she would never push it out. I wanted to at least give her a chance to deliver."

"She was just a baby, herself. At twelve, pregnancy shouldn't even enter her mind, especially *her* pregnancy," I lamented.

"She didn't even know what was happening to her. I'll never forget the terror I saw in her eyes. Oh, and honey, little Melissa was horribly brutalized by that monster. She was so swollen and bruised. It must have happened in the last three or four days."

"I can only imagine how horrible it was for her. No wonder she cried so hard."

"How are you feeling? Tell me the truth. How hard was this for you?"

"I really don't want to answer your question. I'm afraid you'll make me quit."

"That bad, huh?" he returned.

"I promise you I won't harm our babies. I'm exhausted, and I just made it to the bathroom before I threw up, after seeing that little baby. I threw up from Iona's peculiar odor. So I haven't faired so well on my maiden voyage."

"You did remarkably well. When we were working with Hannah, you anticipated our every move, and had things ready when we needed them. I couldn't have asked more of you."

"I was surprised how much of my training came back right when I needed it."

"What I'm going to say next I want you take the right way."

I knew it was going to be something I didn't want to hear by the way it was worded. I could feel myself stiffen for the next sentence.

"I can't worry about you and take care of crises. We made it through today by the grace of God. So…"

He softened his voice as he continued.

"I would like for you to wait until after the babies are born to continue doing this."

My tears came unbidden and I couldn't control them. Daniel pulled me close to him.

"Honey, I didn't mean to make you cry."

"You didn't make me cry. The reason I'm crying is because I know what you're saying is true."

"Maybe we could take some shorter trips and you could go with me on them."

"You think so?"

"Yeah, I think that would be a good idea."

I glanced over Daniel's shoulder at the clock. It was a quarter till midnight. I could tell Daniel was already drifting off when the phone rang. He rolled over with a moan and took the call.

"Dr. Scott."

"Yeah, just now? How is she doing?"

"Oh man, I figured it was going to be a mess. Will she be okay?"

"How is Hannah?"

"Thank you. Chris helped me."

"Badly deformed, he was stillborn."

"I didn't tell her anything. I kept her pretty much out after the surgery. She probably won't remember anything. Her mother? Tell her that her mother is very sick and won't be able to visit, but her aunt Iona will be there tomorrow."

"I agree with you, she doesn't need to know about Melissa."

"Okay, I'll see you tomorrow at the hospital."

"Goodnight."

"I presume that was Roger."

"Yeah, he thanked me for sending him some work," he said with a chuckle. "He just got out of surgery with Melissa. I guess he figured if he couldn't sleep, I couldn't either."

"How's Melissa?"

"He took her straight to surgery. Let's see," he said, turning to look at the clock, "she was in surgery for four hours. She was really damaged, he had to reconstruct her vagina, and also her rectum was torn. She was just ripped apart inside. The infection had traveled all around her insides, but he thinks everything will work okay one day."

"How's Hannah?"

"Hannah is crying for her mama. She still hasn't asked for her baby, but that doesn't surprise me. I think it all is probably like a bad dream to her. He isn't going to tell her what happened to Melissa. He said we did a good job on her. She is stable and comfortable."

"On that good note, I think I'm going back to sleep," he said, kissing me on the forehead.

"Me too." I mumbled as I scooted up close to him.